Battle Scars

Battle Scars

John Wilson

KCP Fiction

KCP Fiction is an imprint of Kids Can Press

This is a work of fiction and any resemblance of characters to persons living or dead is purely coincidental.

Kids Can Press acknowledges the financial support of the Government of Ontario, through the Ontario Media Development Corporation's Ontario Book Initiative; the Ontario Arts Council; the Canada Council for the Arts; and the Government of Canada, through the BPIDP, for our publishing activity.

Published in Canada by   Published in the U.S. by
Kids Can Press Ltd.   Kids Can Press Ltd.
29 Birch Avenue   2250 Military Road
Toronto, ON M4V 1E2   Tonawanda, NY 14150

www.kidscanpress.com

Edited by Charis Wahl
Cover designed by Karen Powers
Cover photo courtesy Library of Congress

Printed and bound in Canada

The hardcover edition of this book is smyth sewn casebound.
The paperback edition of this book is limp sewn with a drawn-on cover.

CM 05 0 9 8 7 6 5 4 3 2 1
CM PA 05 0 9 8 7 6 5 4 3 2 1

National Library of Canada Cataloguing in Publication Data

Wilson, John (John Alexander), 1951–
    Battle scars / John Wilson.

Sequel to: The flags of war.

ISBN 1-55337-702-8 (bound).   ISBN 1-55337-703-6 (pbk.)

I. Title.

PS8595.I5834B38 2005   jC813'.54   C2004-904766-3

For Blaire

NATE

April 26, 1862
McGregor Plantation
Charleston, South Carolina

Something was wrong. The gardens were overgrown, the house paint was peeling, ivy rambled out of control, and even some panes in the upstairs windows were broken. How could the plantation have got so run-down?

Nate McGregor crouched at the end of the drive, looking more like a beggar than a soldier. The soles of his boots flapped mournfully and the dust of many miles hung about him. He was dirty, unkempt and dressed in tattered clothes that were little more than rags. Distant thunder rumbled and the warm air felt heavy and oppressive.

Nate wondered if his father was dead. He knew he had been sick — that was why Nate had made the journey here — and James McGregor's death would explain the run-down look of the place, but when had it happened? Nate had last seen his father at Christmas. If he had died soon after, surely Nate would have heard. If he had died recently, how had the plantation deteriorated so quickly? It didn't make sense.

After about ten minutes, during which nothing moved and the only sound was that of the arguing crows in the overhanging trees, Nate stood up. There was no point in putting it off any longer. He trudged down the rutted, tree-shaded drive and climbed the steps to the heavy front door. Nate had raised his hand to the brass knocker before realizing that the door was ajar. Gently he pushed it open and stepped into the dusty hall, furnished exactly as he remembered it. The doorways leading to the dining room, the study, the kitchen, the stairs curving up to the bedrooms — it was all so painfully familiar. A harsh flash of lightning threw the hallway into stark relief, making Nate jump. It was immediately followed by a rumble that seemed to come from beneath his feet. He headed across the hall toward his father's study.

As he approached the open door, Nate could see the book-lined walls, the fireplace and, to one side, his father's huge desk. It was strangely neat, the papers precisely stacked. Tentatively, Nate stepped into the room.

The door hit Nate a stunning blow on the side of the head and threw him against the wall. An arm wrapped itself around his neck, and the hard edges of twin shotgun barrels felt cold against his temple.

"Didn't I tell you and your thugs never to set foot here again?" a familiar voice said.

"Father!" Nate coughed against the pressure on his throat.

"You can't fool me. Nathaniel's dead at Shiloh. I got the letter. He died a hero. I ought to blow your brains all over the wall."

Nate heard the hammer of the shotgun cock. He struggled to draw in enough breath to talk. "I ran away," he gasped. "I met cousin Walt from Canada."

"Canada?" The grip on Nate's throat loosened.

"Yes, and Sunday. He saved my life."

"Is it really you, Nathaniel?" The shotgun fell away. Nate pulled back and turned.

The figure before him was familiar but, like the house, James McGregor was changed. The hair was still snow white, but it straggled unkempt over the shirt collar. The lines on the face were deep canyons and the always-thin hands seemed almost skeletal. But the most obvious change was in the eyes. They had previously regarded the world with certainty. Now they nervously fled back and forth as if they expected betrayal on every side.

"You're not dead!" The words escaped Nate before he could control them.

A strange smile flickered to life over James's face. "Not yet," he said. "They can't kill me — though they've tried. Oh yes, they've tried, all right. But now you're back, Nathaniel, we will show them what for. My pistol's in the desk drawer. You get it. We've got them bested now for sure. You watch the back of the house. I'll watch the front."

The old man's eyes swung wildly, their movement mimicked disconcertingly by the shotgun barrels. Nate's shock at finding his father alive was rapidly giving way to confusion. "What do you mean?" Nate asked. "Who are they?"

"They!" his father answered loudly. "The Heywards. My own mother's family. They're trying to kill me and take over the plantation. They've already driven all the slaves off with their threats. But they won't scare me so easily." James whispered conspiratorially, "It's Elizabeth, you know."

"What is?" Nate asked in slack-jawed confusion.

"Why, the cause of all this trouble. Things were just fine until your mother had to go and die. Then that man Lincoln gets himself elected and all has gone to hell."

Lightning flashed harshly and deep thunder shook the house around them.

"They're back! They're back!" James yelled wildly, suddenly overwhelmed.

"No!" Nate said. "It's just the storm." But it was no use. His father was oblivious to everything but his mad thoughts.

"You won't get me!" he shouted, raising the shotgun. "Nathaniel's back now and we will defend our home to the death."

Nate lunged at the gun and twisted it aside. He was deafened by the explosion as both barrels went off. A shower of plaster fell around them as a great ragged hole was torn in the high ceiling. The smoking shotgun fell with a dull clatter and James slumped to the polished wooden floor.

He looked frighteningly frail, hugging his knees, rocking back and forth, tears trickling down his cheeks. Over and over he mumbled, "Won't get me now that Nathaniel's home."

As Nate tried to comfort James, the old man was wracked by shuddering coughs, and a bright trickle of blood dribbled from the corner of his mouth.

"Let's get you up to bed," Nate said once the coughing had passed.

"We mustn't let them in!"

"I'm home now. I won't let them in."

James allowed himself to be led upstairs.

Once he was in bed, propped up on a pile of pillows and with the blood cleaned off his chin, he seemed more like his old self. The madness seemed to have passed.

"Why are you back from the war?" he asked Nate.

"I came to see you."

"Before I die?"

"You're not going to —," Nate protested, but his father raised a skinny hand to cut him off.

"Yes, I am. And soon. But I am glad to have this chance to talk with you. I haven't been the best father in the world."

James waved off his son's protest before it began.

"All fathers make mistakes, but without a mother you have probably suffered from mine more than you should have. What I regret most" — Nate waited patiently while a coughing attack passed — "is losing your legacy. Your grandfather Angus built up this plantation to pass to me, and I wanted to do the same for you. Instead, I have lost it all."

James was close to tears. Nate reached over and squeezed his bony hands. "No one can help the war," he said.

James smiled weakly. "Oh, the war didn't help, but the damage was done long before the Yankee blockade stopped the cotton trade. I've never had a good head for business, and I trusted people I shouldn't have. The overseer, Frank King. I trusted him with the book-keeping and he robbed me blind. When it was all gone, he ran off.

"I'm sorry, Nathaniel. There's nothing left but debts. I should have sold out. The Heywards made an offer, but I was too stubborn. I wanted more. But they shouldn't have run off the slaves."

The wild look was back in James's eyes. "They tried to kill me, Nathaniel. But we won't let them get us, will we?"

"No. No." Nate soothed his father until the old man calmed down. "You don't need to worry, Father, everything will be fine. And Frank King is dead."

"Dead?"

"Yes. Do you remember Sunday, the slave who ran away? He killed King just before the Battle of Shiloh."

"Sunday?"

"I met him in the battle. He was fighting for the Union, alongside my cousin, Walter."

"Cousin?" A puzzled expression crossed James's face.

"Yes. The Canadian McGregors — grandfather Angus's brother Lachlan's family. Since the War of Independence they've been living near a place called Cornwall in Ontario. Apparently, Sunday fled to Canada and ended up not far from Cousin Walt. Frank King followed him and tried to recapture him, but couldn't.

"Then King did something I don't understand. He went back to Canada and kidnapped Walt. He had become a crimping agent and sold him to the army. Even King must've seen that was a stupid thing to do — go into a foreign country to kidnap one person. It wouldn't be worth the risk for the small fee. It makes no sense.

"Anyway, Walt and King became part of Nathan Hanson Woods's irregular cavalry. They attacked a baggage train that Sunday was guarding at Shiloh. Sunday killed King and Walt escaped. Later, during the battle, Walt almost killed me but Sunday recognized me and the three of us got away.

"We traveled together for a few days but then Union cavalry found us. I hid, but Walt and Sunday went north. Sunday wanted to join a black unit in the Union army. Walt was headed home.

"Sunday can talk now. Walt taught him some kind of language you make using your hands. Walt's so different from me, yet was like finding a part of myself that has been missing all my life.

"After this war is over, I will go find Walt in Canada and reunite the family. You see, I have a fine legacy — a new family. So you don't have to worry about the plantation."

"There's so much I don't understand," James said wearily. "This war has thrown everything upside down — slaves fighting beside Canadian cousins against my son." The old man shook his head sadly. Gradually, his eyelids drooped and he slept.

May 7th, 1862
Charleston, South Carolina

Dear Walt and Sunday,

There are many things I want to tell you, but I must begin with the saddest.

Father died this morning at about 6 o'clock.

It was peaceful and not unexpected. Since I have returned home, his body and his mind have gone downhill steadily. I tended to him as best I could, but there was nothing anyone could do. I was with him last night, and he had a quiet time, with not too much coughing. I had dozed off in the armchair and, at first, I thought it was the morning sun that had awoken me, but it was the strange silence in the room. His struggle was over at last.

I am glad at least that I arrived here in time. There were moments during these last days when he was lucid and we could talk.

I will bury Father in the small cottonwood grove out back, beside Mother. He would like that. Tomorrow, I will go and sell the plantation to the Heywards. They are my grandmother's family, and Father said they were interested in buying. The plantation is bankrupt, but the sale might pay off the debts and leave enough for me to travel to Richmond.

I am going to join General Longstreet's Corps. There is no doubt the army needs me in these troubled times, but that is not the main reason for my going. I have very little alternative. With the plantation gone, I thought of coming up to Canada to see you both, but that would smack of running away, and I must finish my duty. Death holds little fear for me after what I have seen, and the thrill of battle is undeniable. In any case, they say that, whatever happens, the war will be over soon — by Christmas at the latest. Don't worry about me. I have Judith Henry's sampler from Bull Run to keep me safe.

Perhaps I will come and visit when this is all over. For now, I will say good-bye and good luck.

Your cousin and friend,
Nate

December 7th, 1862
Cornwall, Canada

Dear Nate,

    Your letter from Charleston of May 7 has only just arrived. Who knows where it has been in these troubled times. I suppose it is something of a miracle that it has arrived at all.

    Sunday and I were sorrowed to hear of your father's death. As you said, it is a blessing that it was peaceful — and that you arrived in time.

    Well, it is almost Christmas and the war is not yet over. I wonder what you are doing and where you are. Are you still in the army? I will send this care of Longstreet's Corps at army headquarters in Richmond and hope that they forward it to you. Isn't it strange that I can send a letter to a soldier I was fighting against just this last spring?

    Our news is much less dramatic than yours. After the cavalry found Sunday and me in Tennessee, they took us to Murfreesboro. I wired Father to tell him we were all right, and he wired some money down so we could travel by rail. Even so, it was slow going, made slower by a stop in Montreal to see my mother, and it was June before we finally made it back to Cornwall.

    At first it was wonderful to be safe and sound back at the farm. Sunday moved over to Touss's old place — remember I told you how he was our neighbor who was part of the Underground Railroad and was killed at Shiloh by Frank King? — and I kept busy with the summer work. But when things slowed down in the fall, we both began to get restless. We had seen and done so much that sitting around all winter wasn't appealing.

Sunday came over frequently to visit and practice his sign language and became anxious to get back into the fight against slavery. Mother came to visit in October, and we were sitting on the porch discussing the recent big battle at Antietam and Mr. Lincoln's announcement that the slaves were to be freed.

Mother said she was sure that Mr. Lincoln would allow black men into the army, just to prove that all his fine words about freedom meant something. Sunday signed that he would go tomorrow. Mother said that Boston would be the place to go — they were strong abolitionists there. She has this talent for sweeping statements that seem dumb but have a way of cutting through complexities.

Anyway, she even knew folks there — the Boston Shaws, she called them very grandly. She'd met them years ago when they were all in some sort of commune with famous writers, like Nathaniel Hawthorne and Ralph Waldo Emerson. (She says that Hawthorne was always complaining about the interruptions. What did he expect in a commune?) Apparently everyone got paid a dollar a day whether they worked with their hands or their minds.

To get back to the Shaws, there are Francis and Sarah and they have a son called Robert. Mother wrote them and they invited us down. Robert has been offered command of the first black fighting regiment, the 54th Massachusetts. Sunday is in a fever to join up. I cannot, as only the officers are white and I am not material for an officer, but I shall accompany him and find a place for myself. We are to leave in a few days.

Father is none too keen on the idea, but he accepts my decision. How can I stay here when Sunday has gone? I would feel useless, and the cause is noble enough that I wish to play some small part. And the war cannot go on much longer. The South is near exhaustion and one more good campaign should end it.

So, that is Sunday's and my news. We hope you are well and that this letter reaches you. When this is all over, you are more than welcome to come and stay with us at the farm for as long as you wish. Let us hope that it will not be too far in the future.

If you write again, do so to Father at the farm. He will forward to wherever I am.

Good luck and take care.
Cousin Walt

P.S. Sunday says hello.

N A T E

1:00 p.m., July 3, 1863
Gettysburg, Pennsylvania

Nate leaned his long musket against a tree and gazed out of the woods into the bright sunshine — past the Confederate artillery massed hub to hub along the Emmitsburg Road, across the sloping half mile of plowed fields toward the well-prepared entrenchments on Cemetery Ridge, where Major General George G. Meade's Union Army of the Potomac sat, patiently awaiting their chance to kill him.

In a short while, Nate and the other fifteen thousand men in these woods were going to have to go out into the sunshine, cross the fields and attack Meade's prepared positions. Every man, from General James Longstreet down to the lowliest private, suspected that the coming attack would be the crux of the war. If enough of them lived long enough to take Cemetery Ridge, they would destroy the Union army, and Lincoln would be forced to make peace. However, many guessed that the attack was doomed to fail. Even Longstreet was rumored to have told Robert E. Lee that no fifteen thousand men on earth could take Cemetery Ridge. Lee, who for two years had been outsmarting and running rings around the Union armies, had decided that a different tactic — an all-out frontal assault on the strongest part of the Union line — was what he wanted. And his army would give their beloved general what he wanted — or die trying.

Nate's war had not finished at Christmas. It had dragged on through the bloody fields of Gaines Mill, Antietam, Fredericksburg and back around Judith Henry's now-ruined house at Bull Run.

Nate had been lucky, or perhaps it was Judith Henry's sampler. Most of the soldiers Nate knew had some lucky charm — a rabbit's foot, a letter from a sweetheart, a tear-stained pocket Bible from their mother — that they fervently believed kept them safe, despite the common sight of dead men's bloodstained fingers clutching such tokens. Nate felt in his pocket for the rolled-up cloth that he had taken from the ruined wall of the old woman's house at the first battle of Bull Run, back when the war was still new and exciting. If you had asked him outright, he would have said there was no way a piece of cloth could affect whether a minnie ball smashed his head open or missed him by inches, but deep inside, a part of Nate was sure he would not live long after he was parted from it — and he would fight anyone who tried to take it.

Nate's friend, Jeff, was an exception. He was always teasing Nate about the sampler.

"Won't do you no good," he would say in his broad Tennessee accent. "If'n one o' them minnie balls got yer name 'pon it, t'ain't no piece o' cloth nor paper'll stop it. Only things'll stop a minnie ball's a good sturdy stone wall or split-rail fence."

Nate knew Jeff was right and they both built fences and walls to fight from. But there were no walls or fences on the ground they were going to walk across today — that piece of cloth was his only hope.

Nate looked over at Jeff sitting with his back to a nearby tree whittling a stick with a pocket knife. Jeff was the only person in this war that Nate felt close to — apart from the few days he had known his cousin Walt and Sunday. And both of them might well be dead by now.

Jeff was close to thirty as near as Nate could calculate, but he looked older. A hard life stoking boilers on the Mississippi riverboats and then as a stevedore on the docks at Jacksonville had lined and burned his face well past his years. His short, compact body bore innumerable scars of dropped crates and slipped shovels, and his prominent nose was skewed noticeably to the right as a consequence of a fistfight over some long-forgotten issue. Jefferson Thomas Lutz jokingly claimed that no ball would get him because it could never find a place that hadn't already been injured.

Jeff had befriended Nate in Richmond before Gaines Mill and had shown him the ropes. He had taught him how to coax water from a seemingly dry creek bed and how to forage for food when the army was on the move.

"The importentest thing fer a soldier," Jeff was fond of saying with biblical authority, "is boots. A soldier ain't no good fer nothin' if'n he don't have good feet, and the only sure and certain way to have good feet is to have good boots."

Nate had marched his way through three pairs of good boots, each one taken from a dead Yankee. Boots were worth risking your life for. At Fredericksburg, he had crawled out from the Confederate lines on Marye's Heights to strip the boots from a soldier killed in a Union attack. He had returned, triumphant, but with three musket ball holes in his cap and jacket.

Each time Nate acquired a new pair of boots, he was elated that his feet would be dry and comfortable for a few weeks more, but it depressed him to realize that the army they were fighting seemed to have such an inexhaustible supply of good boots. They had more uniforms, more muskets, more food, more of everything — but it was the wealth of good boots that, for Nate, proved the superiority of his foe.

In fact, it was boots, or the army's need for them, that had led to this battle. Two days previously, some of Stonewall Jackson's old corps had come to Gettysburg because it was said there were Union boots for the taking. But those Union boots had been on the feet of General John Buford's cavalry. The fighting had sucked in the rest of both armies and left thousands of corpses on the fields around the town.

Nate was jerked out of his reverie by an explosion of Confederate artillery. In a flash visible even in the afternoon sun, one hundred and fifty cannons hurled round and explosive shot at the Union lines. Billowing clouds of smoke rose to drift across the view. Almost immediately, the enemy artillery responded. Shells exploded in the woods. A large branch crashed down nearby and small pieces of wood and metal peppered the ground at Nate's feet. Behind him, someone screamed in agony.

"Best be holdin' that piece o' cloth over yer head," Jeff said with a laugh, but Nate ignored him.

This was the time Nate hated most. Once the fighting began, he reacted automatically, did what he was ordered, operated on raw nervous energy. But before the battle, the waiting was excruciating. There was all the fear without any of the action. The dead men that haunted Nate's dreams were the ones killed before the fight — men cut in half by round shot or with their heads blown open by a sharpshooter before they had a chance to get at the enemy. Men killed in an attack often died with expressions of anger or hatred on their faces — more appropriate than the looks of innocence and surprise on those who died before the charge.

Nate huddled down as well as he could, gave himself up to the thunderous rumble of the guns and tried to think of nothing. It was a trick he had learned in his long months as a soldier. Time ran at many different speeds in war. When he was marching hard toward some distant, unknown objective, and when he hadn't eaten for days and his tongue was swollen with thirst and dust, it passed interminably slowly. When he was in a heart-pounding charge toward the flash and smoke of Yankee muskets, time raced by. At times like this, he could empty his mind and just be, for what he thought were a few minutes. Then he would look at his pocket watch and discover that hours had passed.

Nate looked out over the smoke-wreathed fields. The Confederate artillery was still firing away, pounding the enemy lines, but there was no return fire from the ridge.

"Won't be long now," Jeff said.

"Do you reckon the Yankee guns are destroyed?" Nate asked.

Jeff sucked his teeth thoughtfully, adjusted his jacket and tightened the bayonet on the end of his musket. "Nope," he said at last. "I reckon they'll be saving their shot fer us."

The thought sent a chill down Nate's spine. What if the furious barrage hadn't destroyed the enemy positions?

He didn't have a chance to answer his own question. All along the edge of the woods, bugles were sounding and officers on horseback rode into the open. Tentatively at first, and then in gathering numbers, men drifted out and were formed into units. Flags unfurled and flapped lazily in the breeze. The artillery fell silent and the smoke dissipated — giving the Union troops a clear view of the operation in front of the woods. Not a shot rang out. Perhaps they were all dead, Nate thought hopefully.

The men seemed cheerful, some even tossing back

and forth green apples that had been knocked down by the shells. A rabbit jumped in front of Nate and dashed frantically back into the woods.

"Run, old rabbit," Jeff said, "t'ain't your fight. I reckon as if'n I was you I'd be a runnin', too." His comment brought a laugh from several soldiers nearby.

"Come along now, boys," said the officer in charge of Jeff and Nate's company. He was dressed in an immaculate gray uniform, buttons gleaming in the sunlight. He was mounted on a black horse and cantered back and forth in front of his men, encouraging them and waving his saber above his head. "Don't forget that you are from Virginia!"

"I'm from Tennessee," Jeff said under his breath.

"And I am from South Carolina," Nate added.

"Well," Jeff chuckled. "I reckon we'd best show these Virginny boys how some real fighting is done."

Nate felt invulnerable in the midst of this vast forest of bayonets, battle flags and flat caps. So many men — they *had* to be unstoppable.

At last, in the eerie silence after the bombardment, rank upon rank of men, shoulder to shoulder, began a steady walk forward. At the regulation one hundred yards a minute, it would take them nearly nine minutes to reach the Federal lines. The army was like some vast, shiny, spiked insect, half a mile wide, slithering forward over the gentle folds of the ground and up the slope. At first the only sounds were the clatter of equipment, the jangle of the bridles and the heavy breathing of men and animals. The men had been forbidden to run or give the famous rebel yell until they were close to the enemy. Nate felt the hot sun on his neck and cheeks and the annoying prickle of sweat breaking out beneath his coarse woolen uniform. He felt a bit lightheaded, but his musket was comfortingly solid in his hands. With each step, his hopes rose.

One of the first cannonballs from the Union lines decapitated the mounted officer in front of Nate. For a long moment, the strangely headless body, at the whim of the horse beneath it, continued forward, sword splendidly raised in the sun. Then it toppled to the ground.

Solid shot ripped holes in the massed ranks, destroying three or four men at once. Overhead, shells exploded, showering the marching men with deadly fragments and killing or maiming a dozen at a time. Doggedly, they maintained their regular pace, leaning forward against the storm of shot as if it were nothing more than a moderate wind.

Nate and Jeff trudged on. Nate felt the sweat running down his sides and smelled the acrid smoke from the Union cannons. The man in front of him gasped and sagged to the ground. Nate stepped over him. The top of Cemetery Ridge was only about two hundred yards away — two minutes of steady marching, much less in a wild charge. Each stone in the wall in front of Nate was distinct, as were the musket barrels poking over it. In several places, the wall had been pulled down and the black muzzles of cannons stuck out. Nate saw waving blue and gold flags and an officer on horseback who seemed to be looking straight at him.

Then, with an ear-splitting yell, the surviving men surged forward. They made it almost halfway before the massed Union muskets and grape shot-filled cannons went off in unison. An unstoppable weight of lead shot tore into the Confederate ranks. An audible moan, like that of a huge wounded animal, went up from the men. The line staggered to a halt, as if unsure what to do next. They had come eight hundred yards. They had less than one hundred to go — a few seconds for a man running — but it was too far. As the Union gunners and soldiers reloaded and fired into their backs, the beaten army retreated over the bodies of their dead. Some men walked backward, unwilling to show their backs to the enemy. Some fired at the enemy, but it was merely a gesture.

Nate stood and looked at the wall through the swirling smoke. Victory — the end of the war — was only fifty yards away. He felt like crying with frustration.

"Come on!" Jeff yelled in his ear. "Ain't no sense in staying here." He grabbed Nate's sleeve and began pulling him down the slope. Nate resisted — they were so close.

"Come on, you fool!" Jeff shouted at him again. "You'll only git yerself killed standing here."

Killed, Nate thought. Was that what he wanted? Death seemed easy.

All of a sudden, Jeff cursed loudly, lurched and fell face first across the mangled body of a soldier. Forced from his self-absorption, Nate dropped his musket and crouched over his friend. Taking him under the armpits, he lifted. Jeff groaned. He seemed dazed by his fall and held his left arm tightly across his stomach.

"What's wrong with your arm?" Nate shouted as he helped his friend along.

Jeff's only reply was another grunt.

Nate took his friend's good arm, draped it across his shoulder and began an awkward, stumbling run down the hill, half dragging, half carrying Jeff. "The whole Union army's trying to shoot us and you have to fall over and break your arm. Fine soldier you are."

Jeff gasped at each juddering step. He was trying to run, but he seemed strangely uncoordinated.

"It's your arm that's broke, not your legs," Nate said, trying to encourage Jeff, but it was still hard work, and Nate soon stopped talking and worked on in silence.

They reached the trees much faster than they had left them. Nate gently lowered Jeff into a sitting position against a trunk. All around, soldiers, some hideously wounded, streamed through the woods as the few surviving officers attempted to instill some order. Many soldiers, too shocked or exhausted to go on, merely sat looking about with wild, staring eyes.

"You're safe now," Nate said. "We'll rest a minute then go and get that arm set."

Nate looked back over the fields he had just crossed. On the Emmitsburg road, Confederate artillerymen were hitching their guns to horses. Occasional shells burst above them but didn't seem to do much damage. Past the guns, half the soldiers who had set out from the woods only minutes before were scattered like refuse. Some bodies lay in clusters where a shell had exploded.

Others formed a neat line where they had been caught by a musket volley. Still others lay alone. Many were dead, some were too seriously wounded to move, and others staggered or crawled back toward the woods. A low groan, a dull fog of noise, rose as if from the blood-soaked ground itself, occasionally punctuated by a scream of pain or despair.

In front of the Union wall, blue-coated soldiers waved muskets and cheered. Mounted officers galloped back and forth with tattered Confederate battle flags dragging in the dust behind them. Near the center of the front, gray-uniformed prisoners were being herded together.

Nate was awed by the scale of the carnage, but he felt no pity. He and Jeff were alive. And there were things to do. The army would retreat now, and Jeff's arm needed attention.

"I'm cold," Jeff said as if in response to Nate's thoughts.

Nate knelt beside his friend. Jeff was in shock. His face was gray and his eyes were glazed. A worried expression furrowed his brow.

"It's all right," Nate said. "I'll get you a blanket, but we can't stay here. We need to get you to a doctor to set that arm."

"No, I reckon not," Jeff mumbled. His eyes were unnaturally wide and fixed on Nate. A shiver ran through his body. "I reckon there might be somethin' to that piece o' cloth o' your'n, after all," he said with a faint attempt at a smile.

"What do you mean?"

In answer, Jeff looked to where his arm lay over his stomach. His uniform, down as far as his knees, was thickly covered with blood.

"Let me see," Nate said, reaching for Jeff's arm. His friend didn't resist. The arm wasn't broken. Jeff had been holding it across his body to keep his insides from spilling out the jagged tear in his stomach. Nate felt nausea rise to his throat at the sight of gray intestines glistening wetly amidst the dark pulsing blood.

Jeff let out a long sigh and began to shiver. "Ain't … my … arm."

"No," Nate breathed, tears rolling down his cheeks. "But we'll get a doctor to fix you up."

Jeff shook his head feebly. "Best … git … on," he said, through chattering teeth.

As Nate watched, his friend stopped shivering. His body seemed to collapse in on itself and his head lolled. The features that had so often creased in a smile at Nate's pitiful attempts at soldiering or his irrational faith in Judith Henry's sampler went slack.

Nate felt his own being drain away. He had lost everything — his home, his family, his friend — there was nothing left. Anger and guilt surged through him. Anger at the generals who had caused this slaughter, at the war that had destroyed his comfortable life, and at his father, who hadn't been able to protect him. Guilt for his hesitation at the wall across the field, which had cost Jeff his life.

"Why didn't I die instead?" he yelled, grasping his dead friend by the lapels. "Why did you leave me?" Jeff's head rolled foolishly from side to side.

"Damn you!" Nate screamed at the world. "Damn you all!"

He sat, cradling his dead friend as the bloody remnants of the army filed past. As his anger receded, it was replaced by a bleak loneliness — everyone Nate got close to died. His father, Jeff, Judith Henry — probably even Walt and Sunday. The last he had heard was a letter months ago that said they were setting off to join the Union Army. What was the point?

If Nate had been different, he might have surrendered or taken his own life — he had seen soldiers do both — but neither solution was for him. He would go on, but protect himself. Never again would he form a close relationship. No one was going to die and leave him alone again. He would be an automaton — obey orders, march and fight, until he ended up a crumpled, bloody mess in some cornfield.

Wiping his tears, Nate gently laid Jeff on the ground and closed his eyes. He arranged the body as best he could, pulling the torn uniform together and folding the arms across the stomach to hide as much of the horror as possible. Then he took out Judith Henry's sampler, unfolded it and placed it over Jeff's face.

"It's no use to me now," he said. "Saving my life didn't bring me luck." Then he turned and joined the retreat.

WALT

July 15, 1863
New York City, New York

Walt's throat burned as he strained to drag oxygen into his aching lungs. His legs felt like jelly. Soon they would wobble and he would collapse, gasping helplessly. Then they would kill him. And it was all his own doing.

Walt had been walking along Clarkson Street, down by the docks, when he had seen the crowd, several hundred strong — the men, women and children seeming almost festive. This was odd, as the city was in turmoil. For the past few days, since the draft list had been posted beside the casualty lists from Gettysburg, there had been riots and looting in the city. Walt had seen smoke drifting up from several large fires that morning. Conscription was unpopular — especially as those with three hundred dollars could buy their way out — but Walt assumed most people saw the necessity of it and that the police could handle any discontent.

So Walt had pushed his way through the cheering crowd to the oddly quiet center, unprepared for the scene he came upon. A man, dressed in the tatters of a police uniform, huddled at the foot of a wall, his knees drawn to his chin and his arms up to protect his head. A pool of blood was forming among the scattered rocks that lay around him. The only sounds were the cracks as rocks missed their target and struck the wall and the soft groans from the man when something hit him.

Walt was overcome by shock and disgust. "Stop it!" he yelled instinctively.

Some of the crowd stopped, looking up to see who was interrupting their fun. A large disheveled man wearing a leather laborer's apron hefted a broken cobblestone in his huge hand.

"Who says so?" he growled in a broad Irish brogue.

All Walt could think to say was, "You'll kill him."

The big man laughed, a deep, brutal sound. "And then it will be one less cop in this city to protect them money-grubbing slave lovers as want to take away work from honest white laborers. On your way, boyo."

"You cannot kill this —"

"Cannot!" the Irishman yelled. "No man nor boy will tell me what I can or cannot do." With frightening speed, the man drew back his arm and let the cobble fly, hitting Walt a painful blow on the shoulder.

"Kill the cop lover!" a voice screamed. Another rock flew. This one missed Walt and hit a man beside him, who let out an angry curse. The tightness of the crowd and the confusion caused by the flying rocks gave Walt his chance. Pushing his way back through the crowd, he made his escape. Unfortunately, as soon as he was free of the crowd, he stood out, and several men chased him. They were joined by the huge Irishman. Soon, about fifty people were running after Walt. Many could have had no idea why they were chasing the boy, but their blood was up and the chase provided sport. It was enough that someone thought Walt worth chasing. The curses behind him and the pieces of stone skittering along the ground by his pounding feet left Walt with no illusions as to his fate if the mob caught him.

The image of the bloodied policeman kept Walt going, even though his tortured body was screaming that it couldn't go on anymore. His only chance was to get off the street. He raced around a corner and, with the last of his strength, hurled himself against a heavy door, praying it was unlocked. Pain seared through Walt's shoulder; the door refused to give. He was trapped — and exhausted. He slumped, wheezing, in the doorway and awaited his fate.

The mob hesitated as it rounded the corner. The leaders had only to turn their heads to see Walt, when a figure exploded from a doorway farther down the street and sprinted across the road.

In an instant, Walt was forgotten as the mob set off howling after this new prey. Stumbling with terror, the man was run down within the block and fell beneath a flurry of blows.

Jubilant cries of "We've caught a black!" and "Burn him!" brought more and more spectators. Walt, forgotten now, huddled in the doorway and watched.

The big Irishman seemed to be organizing the others. Selecting an overhanging limb on a large tree opposite Walt, the man produced a rope and threw it over. After some activity that Walt couldn't see, the crowd pulled back and heaved on the rope. The black man, clawing at the rope around his neck and twisting convulsively, was being hauled into the air. Every time he managed to gasp in a mouthful of air, the crowd tugged harder and jerked him higher.

Behind the tree, several men were tearing down a low wooden fence and stacking the slats beneath the struggling man. As Walt stared in horror, the bonfire was lit. Once the dry wood was burning fiercely, the black man was lowered slowly down into it. He let out a strangled scream of pain and terror. At this the crowd raised him up. His trousers were on fire and he was kicking his legs furiously. When his clothing was almost burned away, he was lowered into the fire once more.

Each time the man was raised, the burns were worse and his struggles weaker. Each time the crowd cheered. Eventually, the charred body hung limp. Several people poked it with sticks. When this produced no reaction, the rope was tied off, leaving the body to swing above the dying fire. The crowd began to lose interest. A few hurled rocks through the windows of the smarter-looking houses on the street.

The lynching had taken barely fifteen minutes. Walt's throat still hurt and his shoulder was sore where the cobble had hit him, but he knew he would have to make his escape before the mob noticed him again. He was just rising painfully to his feet, trying to decide which way to go, when the door behind him opened and a soft voice said, "You'd best come in."

Without a second thought, Walt slipped through the partially open door and into a dim hallway. The solid latch clicking behind him was the best sound in the world.

It took a moment for Walt's eyes to adjust to the gloom. His savior stood before him, watching quietly. She was a tiny old woman, almost disappearing in a blizzard of lace and bows that looked ridiculously old-fashioned, even to Walt's country eyes. She stood with her hands clasped in front of her, watching Walt like a nervous bird.

"Martha!" A strong female voice emanated from the open doorway on Walt's right. The small woman jumped at the sound. "Bring the boy in here. There's no use rescuing him if we are to hold him prisoner in our hallway. No one will see him through the drapes."

Walt followed Martha and found himself in a high-ceilinged, cluttered room. Every bit of floor supported some piece of furniture: overstuffed floral-patterned armchairs, daybeds, side and sewing tables, a tea trolley, a card table laid out with two hands of gin rummy, an assortment of sideboards and three elephant's feet. Glassed-in bookcases of all shapes and sizes were scattered around the lower walls and, above and between, paintings and sketches hung from the picture rail, leaving barely enough room for the gaslight fixtures.

Every surface, from the large mantel over the

fireplace to the tabletops and the sideboards, was covered with an Aladdin's cave of treasures. Austere green Chinese figures competed for space with fat, smiling Buddhas; ornate, brightly colored vases stood precariously atop carved fragments of Corinthian pillar; severe busts of Roman emperors looked down their noses at many-armed dancing Eastern gods; and a sharp-eyed stuffed eagle stared in eternal frustration from its perch on the highest bookcase at a collection of stuffed rodents and birds.

Walt counted six clocks ticking away, but several more might easily have been hidden in the clutter. A large fire burned in the grate and the room was oppressively hot. It also smelled strongly of cat, and several felines lounged languorously over the furniture. The only human in the room was a large woman in a cane wheelchair to one side of the fire. A huge marmalade cat lay asleep on her lap.

"Come in," the woman said. "Find yourself a seat. Martha has just made tea. May we offer you a cup?"

"Yes. Thank you," Walt said automatically, stunned by the sudden change in his circumstances.

He zigzagged his way to a huge armchair by the fire and sank into its depths, wondering vaguely if he would ever be able to get out. A sleek black cat roused itself from the floor by his feet, stretched and jumped onto his lap, where it curled up and purred contentedly.

"That's Washington," the large woman said. "He likes to be first to introduce himself to visitors. Now, Martha, be so good as to pour our guest a cup of tea, and offer him a slice of your excellent fruitcake.

"You will have a piece," she said, turning to Walt. It was more an order than a request.

"I — I'd love a piece," Walt stammered.

"Good. Good. Now, you must excuse our poor hospitality. I have been stuck in this contraption" — with a regal wave she indicated her chair, which creaked a protest at her movement — "since I was stupid enough to fall off my horse going over a hedge back in — when was it, Martha? — thirty-seven?"

"Eighteen thirty-five," Martha said quietly, in a tone that suggested she had kept track of all the days in between.

"Exactly!" the woman exclaimed as if Martha had confirmed her first statement. "Now, formalities. My name is Jane. Jane Somerway, originally of Blandford Forum on the Stour River in Dorset but, since Father decided to up and seek his fortune in this republic when I was but a tender twelve years of age, a citizen of New York City. And you are?"

"Walter McGregor, but most folks just call me Walt."

"Pleased to meet you, Walt. Now, that is not an accent I recognize."

"I'm from Canada."

"A Canadian boy. Splendid. Now this" — Jane waved expansively to indicate the small woman approaching Walt with a cup and saucer in one hand and a plate bearing a generous chunk of dark cake in the other — "is my sister Martha. Father always said that God miscalculated us. Between us we have enough material for two normal people, but somehow, too much was poured into my mold and too little into Martha's."

Jane laughed heartily as Walt accepted the tea and cake and looked around in vain for a surface to put them on. Eventually, he settled for precariously balancing the cake on the right arm of his chair and holding on to the saucer with his left hand. Still in shock from his escape, but not wanting to appear impolite, Walt gingerly broke off a piece of cake. It was surprisingly good — moist, fruity and very rich.

"So," Jane said, as Martha brought her tea, "what made that rabble think you were worth chasing?"

"I told them to stop stoning a policeman," Walt answered through a mouthful of cake.

"I see. They have a powerful hatred of the police. I really don't know what this city is coming to. It used to be quite a civilized place, at least for this part of the world. Not as cultured as Boston, of course, but less restricted, too. Now these Irish louts rampage through respectable streets, stoning policemen, burning the houses of Republicans and hanging any poor blacks they find."

"It's the draft they hate," Walt said. "They think it's unfair that the rich can buy their way out of fighting while the poor have to go."

"Utter piffle!" Jane exclaimed. "Oh, the draft notices may have triggered this mess, but going into the army would be a step up for most of these louts. No, it's fear of the black man that is driving these troubles. Why, just yesterday a mob marched down this very street chanting for Jeff Davis to become president."

"But we're fighting against slavery," Walt said, puzzled.

"We are, indeed. And a damn good thing, too, but not everyone feels that way. These New York Irish do all the disgusting jobs that no one else will do but are essential for the running of the city. They see thousands of freed slaves arriving and taking away their jobs because they will work for an even more meager pittance than the Irish accept. At the bottom of the heap losing your job means starving, so every poor black man they string up or beat to death is one less threat to their livelihood." Jane paused and absently scratched the ear of the cat on her lap.

"Martha, take a peek through the drapes and see what is going on out there."

Obediently, the tiny woman moved through the obstacle course of mismatched furniture and nervously peered between the heavy velvet folds covering the window.

"That poor man's still hanging there," she said in a voice that Walt had to strain to catch.

"Poor soul. But what mischief is the mob up to now?"

"None that I can see." Martha leaned to see as far down the street as possible. "They seem to be gathered around Senator Carver's house."

"Well, that figures, given his abolitionist sympathies. I hope he has managed to get his little girls somewhere safe." Jane shook her head. "Sometimes I despair for the whole human race, I really do."

A musket shot echoed and made Martha retreat from the window. Instinctively, Walt stood up, spilling tea on the carpet. No one but the cats seemed to notice.

"Oh dear!" Jane exclaimed. "It sounds as if things are getting worse. You'd best take a look, young Walt. But keep your head low."

Walt made his way to the window. Crouching, he pulled the drapes aside slightly and squinted out.

The street was chaos — figures running, some standing, most looking back down the street.

A movement on the opposite roof caught Walt's eye. A man stood, aimed a musket, fired, then ducked back behind the parapet.

Some fifty yards away, a line of about thirty blue-coated soldiers stood across the width of the road. They held their muskets at an angle across their chests. With a gasp, Walt recognized two officers of his own unit, Captain Henry Fleming and Lieutenant Andrew Davis. Captain Fleming was standing to one side, holding his sword aloft and shouting at the rabble.

In the crowd, Walt spotted the Irishman who had first thrown the rock at him. A pistol was pointed at the soldiers, then there was a crash and a puff of smoke. Walt glanced down the street — a soldier had dropped his musket and crumpled to his knees.

Captain Fleming was still shouting, but now he was addressing his own men. The soldiers raised their muskets to their shoulders and disappeared in a cloud of powder smoke.

The roar of the volley brought a gasp from Martha, standing behind Walt, but had a more dramatic effect on the crowd. Instantly, they had become a fleeing mob. In moments they were gone, leaving half a dozen bloodstained bodies, including the big Irishman's, on the ground.

Calmly, the soldiers reloaded their muskets, moved the wounded man to the rear and began a slow march along the street.

"I have to go," Walt said, turning back into the room. "The soldiers have fired on the crowd. It is my unit and I must rejoin them."

"Of course you must," Jane said. "I am glad we could be of help and sorry we had to meet in such terrible times. Perhaps you might come back and visit when this mess is all over."

"I'll do that, and thank you very much. You — and that man hanging from the tree outside — saved my life."

"Nonsense. Now get on with you. Martha, show young Walt back to the war."

Walt followed Martha into the hallway. As she unlatched the door, he had the feeling that he was returning to reality, but what a strange reality it was: he had almost been killed, seen a mob supposedly on the side of abolition brutally murder a black man, and witnessed his own regiment open fire on Union civilians. His father had been right — there was nothing straightforward about this war.

Walt slipped out the door with a quick thank-you to Martha, who smiled and nodded in return. Stepping over the bodies in the street and trying not to look at the mutilated body on the tree, Walt reported to Captain Fleming.

"So, McGregor," Fleming said, "you have rejoined us at a rather opportune moment. Collect the wounded soldier's musket and join us in clearing the streets of this rabble."

"Yes, sir," Walt snapped, relieved to be safe among his colleagues.

July 17th, 1863
Morris Island, Charleston Harbor

Mister Walt,

I is writting this leter on my own without Touss to help me. But I learnt good and you helped a lot last summer.

We was in a battle just two days back in the woods near here, a skermish they called it. I was pretty scared and I think everyone else was too but we done well and drove off them rebels. Tomorrow, they says we has to attack a fort at the end of the island. The 54th has the honor of leeding the attack. Colonel Shaw got us that and he will leed us. The Colonel is a reel good man and we all worship him.

I think tomorrow will be a hard day, so I am writting in case I am kilt. If I am, do not be sory for me. It has been the best time of my life down here fiteing beside other black men. We has shown the world that we kin fite as good as any white men.

Colonel Shaw says that, if I could talk, I would be a Corporal or mabe even a Sargent by now. I have even found one man who can speak the hand language and we talk a lot in the evenings. He is from New York. Elsewise, I just listen.

I must stop now as there is much work to do. Wish me luck tomorow as I wish you luck wherever you are. Take care. Say helo to your father for me if you are writting to him.

I wonder where Nate is now. I often wonder about him.

Good-bye
Your friend Sunday

SUNDAY

July 18, 1863
Morris Island, Charleston Harbor

In the low evening sunlight, the Confederate fort at the far end of the narrow beach didn't look like much. Only some sandbagged gun positions and a few low wooden parapets distinguished the structure from the surrounding sand dunes, but Sunday knew that appearances were deceptive. Fort Wagner was well designed. Its low profile made it a difficult target for both the Union artillery on the island and the gunboats offshore, and the dunes ensured that hits lost much of their force in spectacular but useless geysers of sand. In fact, the fort had been absorbing artillery fire all day without any apparent ill effects.

Moreover, Fort Wagner could be attacked only from the ocean side of the island, and this beach was so narrow that the six hundred attackers of the 54th Massachusetts Regiment were tightly wedged together, an easy target for the thirteen hundred defenders. Sunday reckoned that he and many of his friends would not live to see the night through. Yet, Sunday wished to be nowhere else. No one was forcing him to be in this place or to do things he was about to do. And he was here with others like him.

The 54th Massachusetts had been training for months. For a long time they had no muskets, their pay was less than a white soldier's, and they had been used as little more than beasts of burden, all because many in the Union army believed that black men did not have the intelligence, courage or character to perform well in battle. Now they were getting their chance to show what they could do. If they captured Fort Wagner, the door would open to tens of thousands of other black volunteers eager to shorten the war and end slavery.

Sunday was proud as he stood on the beach with the sun setting over his left shoulder and the restless swell of the Atlantic sparkling on his right. But he was also scared. When the Confederacy had announced that any black man captured in uniform would be shot, Colonel Shaw had offered any man in the 54th who wanted it an honorable discharge — not one man had accepted. Later, Sunday discovered that white officers captured while leading black troops were also to be executed.

Colonel Robert Shaw now stood in front of his soldiers, surveying the fort through a telescope. Sunday and Walt had called on the Shaws, as Walt's mother had suggested, when they were in Boston — Shaw had been at home recovering from a neck wound.

At first Sunday had been overawed by these white folks whose grand life was very similar to that of slave owners, but he soon began to see differences. Plenty of black men and women attended to the Shaws' needs, but they were paid servants, not slaves. They had uniforms, their own quarters, and they could come and go as they pleased in their spare time.

Other black men came to visit and were treated the same as any white guest. Sunday remembered one in particular, a large man with stern eyes, a mop of frizzy hair and a neatly trimmed beard flecked with gray. Like Sunday, Frederick Douglass was an escaped slave. Unlike Sunday, he could talk, in a deep, rich voice that he used to great effect.

Douglass could not understand Sunday's sign language, but that didn't prevent him from having one-sided conversations with him. The first time they met, Douglass told Sunday a long involved story about how the white antislavery activist John Brown had invited him to go along on his famous raid to begin a slave uprising. Douglass had refused because he thought, correctly, that Brown's plan was suicidal, but now he regretted it. "His zeal in the cause of freedom was infinitely superior to mine," Douglass told Sunday. "I could live for the slave — John Brown could die for him."

Sunday was impressed by Douglass's way with words. On New Year's Eve, he went with hundreds of others, black and white, to the Music Hall in Boston to celebrate Emancipation becoming law. From the low stage, Douglass had addressed the crowd.

"I am here this night as a thief and a robber," he said. "I stole this head, these arms and legs and this body from my master and ran off with them. But from tonight, no one need be a thief anymore in order to gain control over their body. Our sons and daughters, wives and husbands can no longer be sold out of our families. We are free."

The crowd erupted in wild cheering. As it subsided, Douglass went on. "And there is someone in this audience who, ten years ago, wrote a book that has done more than any of the rest of us could to bring the cruel horrors of slavery to the minds of millions." He raised a hand to point to the balcony at the back of the hall. "Miss Harriet Beecher Stowe, the famed author of *Uncle Tom's Cabin*, stand and let us thank you."

As one, the crowd turned and looked up as a small white woman, dressed in black and with tears streaming down her cheeks, stood and waved at the mass of people below her. Sunday wished he could join in the cheers. *Uncle Tom's Cabin* was one of the first books he'd learned to read, and here was the author.

When Sunday thought about it, and he did often, he could barely believe how his life had changed because of the war. From being a slave brutalized by the overseer, he had become a man and volunteer soldier. He had discovered friendship — with Walt and his father, Kenneth, and Touss. He had even met the son of his old owner on equal terms in the heat of battle. From being locked in silence and ignorance, he had learned to read and write and communicate. He had devoured every book he came upon to learn everything he could. He would never know it all, but discovering new things thrilled him.

Of course this new freedom brought a responsibility that Sunday felt strongly, the responsibility to give the freedom he had to others — and it was a responsibility that might end his newly free life very shortly.

Colonel Shaw turned to face his men. "Remember, you are but six hundred, but tens of thousands will look on what you do tonight. You fight as free men, so that others may also be free.

"Move in quick time until you are within a hundred yards of the fort. Then, double-quick and charge. Do not stop for a comrade, but if the standard-bearer should fall, who will pick up the flag to place it upon the enemy battlements?"

"I shall," a dozen voices answered at once.

"Good," Shaw replied. "Then let us go."

At a steady pace, the 54th moved behind their colonel along the beach. The sand was firm underfoot and the evening was hot. The sights and sounds of the charge assaulted Sunday's senses, but he felt distanced from them, as if he was reading about the battle in a book. He felt strangely calm. Even when the shelling began and his friends dropped to the sand, he registered the information and kept going, automatically, marching when he could and removing wire and branch obstacles when he had to. All the time, he kept his eyes on Shaw out in front.

After what seemed an age, Sunday found himself in a deep crater. All around him, men hugged the ground or tried to rise and fire their muskets. But the gunfire was too hot. In front of Sunday, the sand sloped up to the sandbagged fort. On the parapet, soldiers in gray uniforms methodically fired down into the mass of attackers. Some shouted taunts. "Yankees must be getting desperate, sending blacks to do their fightin' for them. But we can kill slaves as easy as Yankees."

"We must not stay here!" Shaw yelled.

Standing, he began a stumbling run up the slope. The flag-bearer followed him, leading those who weren't shot down as soon as they stood.

Sunday was soaked in sweat. His lungs ached and his eyes felt on fire from the sand under his lids. But he ran on.

Looking up, he saw Shaw reach the parapet and fire his pistol down into the fort. The flag-bearer stood beside him, waving the banner to encourage the others. More and more men were reaching the parapet and firing down the other side. We've done it, Sunday thought as he struggled through the soft sand. Then Shaw disappeared. One moment he was standing there, then he was gone. Sunday struggled on, as much to find out what had happened to the colonel as to take the fort.

The sight at the top took his breath away. Behind the parapet was another, lined with soldiers busily shooting at anyone who approached. The space between was littered with the dead of both sides. Sunday glimpsed a white body in a blue uniform before something hit him on the side of the head. He felt himself falling.

Sunday was wrapped in darkness, wrapped so tight that he couldn't move. For what seemed an eternity he had fallen, down through the battle and the night, until he reached the very center of the earth. Now he was still. He could hear the shells bursting above him, but they shed no light. He could hear men shouting, running, dying, but they were on the other side of the blackness.

Sunday had no idea whether what he heard was happening immediately after he was hit or a million years later. Was he dead? Was this the spirit world that some of the slaves had talked about?

Voices echoed around in the darkness. Sunday recognized Frederick Douglass, Walt, Touss and Frank King, but the other voices must have been part of the battle that seemed to ebb and flow around him.

"They're over the wall!"

"Turn that cannon!"

"Here they come again!"

After what might have been a few hours or a hundred years, the sounds of fighting faded. Even the blackness seemed to fade to a gray wall between Sunday and the world. Sunday found that he could move his limbs a little. He could feel his fingers and toes and sense painful weights on different parts of his body. Gradually realizing that he might not be dead, Sunday began to struggle.

"This un's movin'!" a voice shouted.

"If he can work, put him over by the others. If not, shoot him."

Sunday felt hands dig under his armpits and pull him from his prison. It was a tremendous relief. Sunday moved his arms and legs experimentally. They appeared to work, but he still couldn't see.

Sunday was standing now, but very unsteadily. The ground beneath him was uneven, and he was afraid to move his feet in case he fell back into whatever had held him for so long. He moved his arms around, seeking something solid to hold on to.

"Oh, shoot, he's blind," a voice said. "Ain't no use."

Sunday heard a flintlock being primed. Frantically, he tore at his eyelids. Flakes of something were coming away beneath his nails. One lid lifted a little, then the other. His hands were covered with dried blood — that was what had sealed his eyes shut, blood from the wound he must have got to his head, which did hurt now.

Sunday looked up. It was daylight, but smoke and low cloud dulled the sun. He was standing at the bottom of the moat between the two parapets. Bodies were heaped all around, and gray-clad soldiers moved here and there, prodding the bodies. When they got a response, they either sent the man to join a pitiful group of ragged survivors standing to one side or put a musket ball into his skull.

"This un ain't blind after all," the man said almost regretfully as he lowered his musket.

"Then get him over with the others, and be quick. We got a lot o' burying to do afore the day gets too hot."

The man waved his musket toward the other prisoners. Sunday's head was pounding, his limbs were stiff and sore, and he was seriously disoriented, but he stumbled over as best he could.

There were about a dozen black soldiers in the group Sunday joined. Most of their uniforms were torn and bloodied, and all looked around nervously. Sunday recognized none of them.

"You men," a Confederate officer shouted, "give them blacks shovels and get them digging!"

For much of the morning, Sunday and the others worked digging deep pits in the soft sand below Fort Wagner's walls. Around midday, when the sun had burned off the high clouds and was beating down mercilessly, they were given a drink of water and told to load the hundreds of bodies into the pits.

It was grim work, especially when Sunday recognized a dead soldier, but the men worked on in silence. Without any discussion, the men worked around the body of Colonel Shaw. At last, in the late afternoon, Shaw's was the only body left. The pits were almost full.

"Take that one, too," the officer said. "If he wants to fight with slaves, he can be buried with them."

Sunday and another man lifted Shaw and carried him to the pit. As gently as possible, they let the body slide down the side, to rest beside the standard-bearer who had accompanied him onto the parapet. Immediately, Sunday and the others were ordered to fill in the mass graves. It was as if Sunday were burying a part of himself. Shaw had been like a father to the black soldiers. He had turned them from ragged, angry ex-slaves into an efficient fighting unit with pride and self-respect.

Sunday knew now that whatever happened, he would never submit to being a slave again — the war and Colonel Shaw had given him that. But the battle at Fort Wagner and the death of Shaw had also given Sunday doubt. Was a war, even a just one, worth the death of a man like Shaw?

The burying was hard work, but Sunday was relieved to be doing it. He had assumed that when the bodies had all been moved to the pits, he would join them. His future was still uncertain, but at least he might survive another night.

During the following few days, under constant shelling from the Union batteries, Sunday and the other men were worked every hour of daylight re-pairing the fort's defenses. They were given occasional sips of water and stale bread twice a day. At night they were shackled so tightly together that it was impossible for them all to lie down at once.

Two men collapsed under the strain and were taken away; three more were killed by an exploding shell. The survivors were roused late one night and herded onto a boat. Lying in the hull, shivering as cold seawater and the blood of four wounded Confederates soaked into his ragged clothes, Sunday contemplated a bleak future.

W A L T

August 2, 1863
Baltimore & Ohio Railroad, Virginia

Outside the window, the Shenandoah Valley unrolled like an endless picture punctuated by occasional clouds of black smoke from the engine's tall smokestack. The afternoon had become uncomfortably hot since the train had passed through the Blue Ridge Mountains at Harper's Ferry. Even though the carriage windows were open and Walt had taken off his jacket, the heat was oppressive. What air did move over Walt and his companions was filled with dust and soot that left long black streaks when they tried to rub them off.

The carriage Walt was in had been coupled to the end of a supply train heading south toward General Rosecrans's Union army at Murfreesboro. General Lee's army, battered but intact, had passed this way only a couple of weeks before on its southern retreat from Gettysburg, and the countryside was far from secure.

Yet cutting across the northern end of the Shenandoah Valley was a faster route from New York to Rosecrans than the safer ramble through Pennsylvania and Ohio.

The men in the carriage were the unit Walt had found on the streets of New York. At the front of the carriage, Captain Fleming and Lieutenant Davis were sprawled on benches, apparently asleep. The rest dozed, sitting upright, two or three to a bench, all being rushed south to rejoin their regiment for the push on Chattanooga.

Walt kept his eyes half closed and tried to ignore his discomfort. He told himself one more time that this was better than marching. At first it had been, but after hours of bruising, aching, bumping, rattling and being stopped in the middle of nowhere, he wasn't sure.

Walt was happy enough to be back among his comrades and returning to his regiment, but the events of New York still troubled him. He couldn't blot out the image of the body of the black man swinging forlornly above the fire. Every time he closed his eyes and most nights when he fell asleep, the horror returned.

Walt had seen many dead men, but this killing haunted him. In the heart of the North, the mob had been just as brutal and racist as Frank King cutting out Sunday's tongue.

Walt had joined the fight, fueled by Sunday's and the Shaws' enthusiasm for the crusade against slavery. Now he wasn't so sure. Were all the dead men worth it if all they died for was the mob?

"I sure hope we get some furlough in Nashville." A voice interrupted his reverie.

"Damned right," a man behind Walt replied. "'Nother three days o' this and I ain't gonna be fit to fight nobody."

Walt doubted that was true. From what he had seen of the men in his carriage, they were prepared to fight anyone — New York Irish laborers or Confederate soldiers — at the drop of a hat.

"Well," a man across the aisle said, "I'm ready. If'n fightin' keeps me off'n this train, I'll chase Johnny Reb clear into Atlanta."

Several men laughed. "Don't you be gettin' too all fired cocky," the man behind Walt said. "Them Rebs ain't beat yet, not by a long shot."

"Sure they are," the second man said. "Why, they was whipped twice, at Gettysburg and Vicksburg, in but two days. All them boys want is to git on back to their farms. And I am surely prepared to encourage them in that endeavor."

"Nope. I won't rest easy 'til ol' Gen'ral Lee's safely behind bars."

At the mention of Lee the men fell silent. Even after Gettysburg, his name was magic. No Northern soldier relished coming up against his army.

"I hear them black boys of the 54th Massachusetts got whipped over by Charleston a couple weeks back," the soldier behind Walt said.

"The 54th! What did you hear about the 54th?" Walt turned so fast that the man beside him complained loudly.

"Well, you're powerful interested. Friendly with the blacks, are ya?"

Walt ignored the question. "What have you heard?"

"Well," the soldier said, spitting loudly, "I heard they was told to attack some fort on an island. Most of 'em was killed.

"Mind," he went on grudgingly, "I did hear as how they fought as brave as white troops. Got themselves into the fort afore they was all killed."

"Well, I say good luck to anyone who fights agin the Rebs," the man across the aisle broke in. "Don't make no difference to me if'n they was black, white or yellow, long as they made sure that there was a few Rebs who won't be around to shoot at me."

Walt slumped back onto his bench. The 54th — Sunday and Robert Shaw. He had learned not to believe all soldiers' gossip, but it seemed certain the 54th had suffered heavy casualties in some attack or other.

Walt was engrossed in his worry about Sunday when the train jerked suddenly to the left. Surprised shouts erupted all through the carriage. The air was filled with the scream of protesting metal. Walt clutched the window ledge for dear life as the tilt increased. The view out the window had changed from landscape to sky.

"We've derailed!" someone shouted.

Everything seemed to happen in slow motion, but Walt could not make sense of it. Windows were shattering, bags and equipment were hurtling all around, and up was becoming down, all to the sound of screeching, tortured metal, splintering wood and the terrified howls of men whose arms and legs were being broken as they were tossed around.

Walt's grip on the window was ripped off and he felt himself falling. He had an extraordinarily clear image of the carriage ceiling being ripped open and grass appearing through it before something he did not see collided with the side of his head and a merciful blackness overwhelmed the chaos.

❖❖❖

"Colonel Woods, sir." The voice was coming at Walt from a long way away. "This here carriage is full of blue-bellies."

"Well, round up the ones that ain't dyin' and we'll take 'em to General Lee. Personally, I'd prefer to shoot 'em, but if they ain't black, I guess we can't."

Walt's first thought was that he was dreaming, which was a great relief; he gave in to a relaxed curiosity about what would happen next. He was engulfed in a variety of strange noises that made no sense. The thump and crash of heavy objects being moved mixed with the creak of wagons and the jingle and stamp of restless horses. Voices shouted unintelligibly, flames crackled nearby — all against the angry hiss of escaping steam.

Quite the dream, but something wasn't right. Walt couldn't see anything, and dreams usually had pictures. And the dream was incredibly vivid. He could smell wood smoke, feel the hot sun on his face and taste the saltiness of blood. Walt could have sworn he was lying on grassy ground and that the strange tickling on his cheek was leaves moving in the breeze. The odd thing was, he seemed to have taken his shirt off, as he could feel blades of grass tickling his skin.

With an incredible effort of will, Walt opened his eyes. The branches of a low bush waved above him; behind it, the puffy white clouds of a summer afternoon scudded by. He seemed to be lying on a gentle grass-covered hill, his head lower than his feet. An exploration with his tongue pinpointed the cut on his cheek that was causing the bloody taste. Walt turned his head to spit and two things happened — a searing pain exploded behind his eyes and he saw the body of Lieutenant Davis lying about ten feet away, the back of his head crushed. Captain Fleming was kneeling over him.

The shock made Walt sit up. Waves of pain made him close his eyes, but he remained upright. He was beginning to remember — a lurch, a screeching of metal, yes, a train wreck. Very slowly, he looked around.

Walt was sitting on a slope below the railbed. He must have been thrown from the carriage and rolled some way down the hill. The ground between Walt and the tracks was littered with what was left of the train. The carriage he had been in lay on its side, its roof ripped open and its contents spilled toward him. Equipment, muskets, broken benches and sprawling bodies — some incomplete — covered the ground. A few men were sitting or standing in a daze, trying to make sense of what they saw.

What remained of Walt's carriage was still attached to a burning goods wagon, the smoke obscuring what must have been the view along the train to the engine.

Walt also slowly realized that he was naked from the waist up. His chest and sides were covered with tiny scratches, many leaking trails of blood down his pale skin. All that remained of his shirt was the lower part of one sleeve and a few tattered strips hanging forlornly from the collar.

As if noticing his injuries had made them real, the scratches began to itch and sting. Walt gingerly touched a few and winced with the pain.

"Here." Walt looked up to see Fleming holding out Lieutenant Davis's jacket. "Put this on. He won't be needing it, and it'll get cold tonight."

Numbly, Walt accepted the jacket. It was still warm from Davis's body. The rough material irritated his skin, but he was glad to have it.

"On your feet, Yank."

Very slowly, Walt turned to look in the opposite direction. Two soldiers in Confederate gray were walking across the slope. One carried a musket and the other a Colt revolver; they were kicking the bodies littering the ground. Those capable of walking were being herded into a small group beside the carriage remains. Before the closest man reached them, Walt struggled to his feet. Every inch of his body hurt, but it was the waves of pain washing through his head that threatened to push him back to his knees. He noticed that Captain Fleming was favoring his left arm and that a dark patch of blood was forming below his elbow.

"Are you all right, sir?" Walt asked.

"I believe so," Fleming replied. "Just a flesh wound. You look as though you have taken a good blow to the head."

Carefully, Walt explored his painful face. His left cheek was sticky with blood and a large lump had formed above his ear, but he could move his jaw and it didn't appear that his skull was broken.

"It's not much," he said.

Fleming nodded. Encouraged by a prod from the revolver, the pair made their way to join the group of survivors.

Only a dozen of the thirty soldiers who had been in the carriage were capable of walking, most sporting some injury or another — the others already dead or too badly injured to walk. They were herded through the smoke toward the front of the derailed train.

Every carriage had left the tracks, although some stood, looking relatively complete, beside the rails. Others were entirely demolished and their contents scattered — hundreds of pairs of boots were spread over the slope, like shiny black rocks.

Remarkably, the engine was still upright, surrounded by clouds of escaping steam, the terrified fireman and engineer standing beside it, holding their hands in the air. Walt noticed that the steel rails were missing for some distance in front of the engine, explaining the derailment.

Among the open carriages and scattered supplies, fifty or so Confederate soldiers were loading as much as they could onto a half dozen wagons at the bottom of the slope. Beside the wagons, a familiar figure sat on horseback shouting orders, someone Walt hadn't seen since he had been kidnapped by Frank King and Jake Stone and forced to fight in his irregular cavalry. He would have been happy to never again set eyes on Nathan Hanson Woods. Chaotic images flooded Walt's mind: Woods's attack on the baggage train at Shiloh, Touss dying, Sunday killing Frank King, and the stranger who turned out to be his cousin Nate, in Confederate gray, leaping the split-rail fence. His past was coming back to haunt him.

Walt wasn't concerned that Woods would recognize him from their brief encounter the year before, but the man was brutal and Walt doubted that his prisoners' lot would be a happy one.

"Hurry it along, boys!" Woods shouted. "I ain't too comfortable bein' this far north. There's no telling when some blue-belly patrol might come along, and we want to put some miles between this wreck and us before the sun sets this night. There's no use helping ourselves to all this good equipment if the Yankees just come and take it back."

Woods glanced at the prisoners. "Bring that sorry lot down, tie their hands, and hitch them to the wagons. A bit of exercise will do them good. If any of them give you the least trouble, shoot 'em."

Walt and the others were herded to the wagons and tied, one man at each corner, to the tailgates. Obviously, they were going to have to walk — run if the wagons sped up — to wherever the raiders were headed.

Walt did not relish the prospect, but what made the chill run through him was another sight from his past: Jake Stone, still heavily bearded, but now wearing the uniform of a Confederate corporal. Walt had had little to do with Stone after he and King had kidnapped Walt and Sunday from the Cornwall farm and sold them into Woods's unit, but no companion of King's could be pleasant. What's more, Stone might recognize Walt and bear him a grudge over King's death.

As Jake worked his way closer, Walt kept his eyes on the dust in front of his feet. Eventually a pair of new boots entered his view. Walt held his hands out to be tied. The man in front of him hesitated. Almost against his will, Walt looked up to find Jake staring at him intently. Then he ran his eyes over Walt's officer's uniform and busied himself tying Walt's hands and fixing the rope to the wagon. When he moved on to the next man, Walt wondered what Stone's silence had meant.

"This is unacceptable." Captain Fleming's voice rose above the creaking of the wagons and the stamping of the impatient horses. "We are prisoners of war — soldiers captured in uniform — and entitled to be treated as such. Some of my men are badly injured. They should have their wounds attended to and be carried on the wagons, not left to die like dogs."

Woods rode down the line and stopped beside Fleming. He glared hard, but Fleming met his stare and held it. Jake had been tying Fleming to the wagon behind Walt's and had stopped to see what would happen. The man at the other corner of Fleming's wagon stood with his head down, swaying uncertainly from side to side. He was heavily favoring his left leg, which had a growing patch of blood on the trousers above the knee.

"So, your blue-belly soldiers ain't got it in them to keep up with good Confederate boys?" Woods asked.

"Not when you are on horseback and we are walking," Fleming replied.

Woods nodded thoughtfully. "And this one" — he inclined his head toward Fleming's injured companion — "you reckon he can't keep up?"

"Of course not. His leg is injured."

Woods nodded again. "I agree with you," he said quietly. Woods drew his long Colt revolver, cocked the hammer and shot the injured soldier in the head. The man collapsed like a sack of beans and lay in the dust in a growing pool of blood.

Woods turned back to Fleming. "I appreciate your assistance. My concern is speed, not mollycoddling prisoners. I will take you all to General Lee. The men who live long enough will be transferred to Belle Isle. As officers, you and your friend" — Walt opened his mouth to deny it but was silenced by a stern look from Fleming — "will be transferred to Libby Prison in Richmond. I dare say, after a few weeks there, you will look back with fondness on the journey you are about to undertake. Now, are there any other men you think will not be able to keep up?"

Fleming shook his head.

"Good," Woods said, holstering his gun, "then we can be on our way. Move out!" he shouted, cantering to the head of the line. Walt was jerked forward as the wagon began to roll.

NATE

August 15, 1863
Orange Court House, Virginia

The Union prisoners sat huddled in a clearing by the road, trying to be invisible. They were filthy, many dressed in rags. None had boots and several had blood-stained cloth roughly tied around old, festering wounds. Some passing soldiers looked at them pityingly. Others cursed and spat. A few guards lethargically warned away anyone who approached too close. An officer stood to one side, engaged in conversation with a tall, bearded corporal.

Nate hesitated at the edge of the trees, no longer sure he had made the right decision. When an officer was looking for an escort to take officer prisoners to Richmond, Nate had volunteered immediately. The retreat from Gettysburg had been long and exhausting, and Nate was thoroughly sick of the soldier's life. All the waiting and marching led only to death and destruction, and the war was no closer to ending.

On top of that, Nate was achingly lonely. Everyone close to him was dead or lost. Nate just wanted to go home — but he had no home to go to. At least in Richmond he would be away from the army for a time, and who knew what opportunity might arise. Shrugging, Nate crossed the clearing.

"Begging your pardon, sir," he said to the officer. "I've been assigned to guard the prisoners."

"Are you all there is?" the officer asked.

"Yes, sir."

"Damnation. I know we are short of men, but two to guard fifteen is madness."

"I don't reckon they'll give us no trouble," the bearded corporal said. His voice was oddly soft coming from such a large frame. "Sir," he added, after the officer threw him a hard stare.

"Very well. There is nothing we can do about it, anyway. Keep them tied and keep a close watch on them. The officers are in that group over yonder to the left. Separate them out. It's a good five miles to the train station, so you'd best be getting them moving."

"Yes, sir," the bearded man said.

The officer gave them both a last long look and marched off.

"Now," the bearded man said as soon as the officer was out of earshot, "I ain't no fancy officer, just a corporal. But don't go makin' the mistake o' thinking that I ain't the one in charge o' this little venture."

As he talked, the man moved to the group of prisoners and kicked the man closest to him.

"Come on, you lazy blue-bellies. You ain't officers

here no more. Time we was a movin'. We got oursel's a train to catch."

Some of the prisoners stirred and struggled to their feet. A few merely looked up disconsolately.

"I aim to get to Richmond," the bearded man said over his shoulder to Nate. "These boys are my ticket, but I only need one. If any gives me trouble, I will shoot him as slick as you like and then I will ask what the trouble was.

"My name's Jake Stone. What's your'n?"

"Nate. Nate McGregor."

"Nate! Is that you?"

One of the prisoners was on his feet, looking hard at Nate. It was the lieutenant's uniform that confused Nate. His cousin was filthy and thinner than when he had last seen him and Sunday riding away with the Union patrol, and he had been a private then. But there was no mistaking.

"You know this blue-belly?" Jake asked.

"Yes," Nate replied. Everyone waited for him to say more, but Nate was overwhelmed. Walt! Alive! Nate was thrilled to rediscover this relative who had crashed into his life so unexpectedly at Shiloh. But it was a thrill he didn't want. Everyone Nate had contact with seemed to die. The last thing he wanted was responsibility for Walt's imprisonment — and possible death.

"He's my cousin," Nate eventually added sullenly.

Jake stared at Nate intensely. "Well, I'll be damned."

Jake's gaze made Nate feel uncomfortable. Surely it wasn't that unusual to have a family split by the war, especially here in Virginia, where half the state supported the Union and the other half the Confederacy.

"I expect there'll be time aplenty for family reminiscences on the road." Jake chuckled. "But right now we'd best be moving along. We'll keep this sorry lot tied in line by the ankles. You lead and I'll come up behind. If'n you hear me holler, you turn around ready to shoot. Understand?"

"Yes," Nate muttered.

"And take good care of your cousin." Jake smiled oddly at Nate. "Prisoners is valuable commodities." He returned to kicking the men to their feet, placing Walt at the front of the line.

"It's good to see you again." Walt's voice came from behind Nate as the line began trudging down the road to town. "When Sunday and I rode off with that patrol, I thought I'd never see you again."

"It'd be just as well if you hadn't," Nate said angrily.

"What do you mean?"

"I mean I'm bad luck."

"Nonsense."

"Is it?" Nate turned and glanced at Walt. "I jinx everyone I come in contact with. You'd best keep away from me."

"I don't believe in jinxes."

"You'd better. I'm taking you to a prison camp. Do you have any idea what those places are like?"

"No."

"If there's a hell on earth, it's them. Andersonville is a disease-ridden open sewer. The inmates kill one another for scraps of food, and there's no water other than a stream that's also a toilet. The bodies are piled outside the gates each morning. But you seem to be an officer now, so you'll be sent to Libby Prison in Richmond. I hear it's better there — only five or six men die of starvation and sickness each week."

Walt fell silent at the bitterness in his cousin's voice.

"Of course," Nate went on, "none of it is deliberate. It's the blockade. If you want to blame someone, blame General Grant cutting off supplies from the west.

"Southern women and children are going hungry. Why waste food on useless prisoners when it could be feeding families and our soldiers fighting for the country's survival?"

Nate seemed to have exhausted his anger for the moment, so the line marched on in silence.

Eventually, Walt tried again. "I got the letter about your father. I was sorry to hear the news. So was Sunday. Did you receive my letter?"

Nate just grunted, so Walt told him the details of what had happened to him and Sunday after Shiloh. He ended with the train wreck and his capture, but didn't mention knowing Jake Stone. He still didn't know why Stone hadn't said anything about him not really being an officer and didn't want to jeopardize his secret.

As Walt talked, Nate's shoulders were becoming more hunched, as if a heavy weight were being transferred onto them. When Walt talked about returning to the farm at Cornwall after the war, Nate turned on him angrily.

"There isn't going to be an 'after the war.' This is a new kind of war. No one wins. Who won Shiloh, Antietam, Gettysburg? Sure, one army or the other retreated, but it was ready to go at it again a few weeks later. Battles don't win wars anymore. This war is just going to grind on forever until there are no soldiers left to fight and no homes left to go to."

Nate's long suppressed anger surprised even himself. He was angry at Judith Henry for stubbornly staying in her house in the middle of a battle, angry at Jeff for staying beside him at the wall at Gettysburg and angry at his father for losing the plantation — and his mind. Most of all, he was angry at himself for not being able to change any of it. The anger, bottled up so long within Nate found a target in Walt, appearing from his past. Nate knew that it made no sense — he should be happy to see his cousin, but he wasn't. As he led the prisoners down the road, his rage fed on itself and he tugged savagely on the rope.

"Damn you, Walt," he spat. "Why did you have to come back into my life? Couldn't you have gone and got yourself killed like I thought?"

At the back of the line, Jake Stone smiled.

SUNDAY

August 18, 1863
Richmond, Virginia

The man in front of Sunday stumbled to one knee on the rough ground, dropping his load of stakes. Knowing what was coming, he immediately curled into a ball and covered his head with his arms. A long whip snaked out and cut a red slash across the man's shoulder.

"Lazy good-for-nothing. Pick up them stakes and get on. You ain't here to lie around all day."

Sunday kept his head down, careful not to meet the eyes of the guard wielding the whip. His bundle of stakes dug painfully into his shoulder, but he stood patiently as the man in front collected his load, hauled himself to his feet and moved on.

There were at least twenty slaves in the line, barefoot and chained by the ankle. Each carried a load of wood picked from the wagon train behind them to be hauled to the earthwork defenses in front. Other gangs of chained men dug trenches and drove in the stakes to shore up the parapet and parados.

It was brutal work, but Sunday took comfort in two things — he had been kept alive even though he was black and captured in uniform, and the frantic work he was being forced to do on the fortifications showed how desperate the Confederates were becoming. The war was obviously not going their way. Sunday's goal was to keep out of trouble and try to stay alive until he either could escape or the Union army arrived to end the war. He hoped the end would come soon — he had heard of the great battle the month before. Surely the Union army, perhaps with Walt, was marching south to capture the enemy capital.

Sunday dropped his pile of stakes by the trench and turned to collect another. The ankle shackles required him to keep in step and move at the same speed as the man in front of him. The work was grueling but its grinding monotony was worse. Since Sunday had discovered the world of reading, monotony had become hard for him to take. In the army, at least it served a good cause, but here, boring work that undermined that cause was almost unbearable.

To occupy his mind, Sunday thought about the two men he admired most — one black, one white, both dead — Robert Shaw in an unmarked mass grave in Fort Wagner and Touss by Frank King's hand at Shiloh. Sunday had thought he wanted nothing more than to live like Shaw, brave and devoted to a noble cause. After the tragedy of Fort Wagner, he wasn't sure. Now, Touss's life, a free man in charge of his own destiny and quietly helping others, seemed more enviable. There had been too much killing. Sometimes Sunday dreamed of returning to Cornwall and taking over Touss's farm, working it until he was old and gray. But first he had to get there.

"That one there." It took Sunday a minute to realize that the man with the whip was referring to him. The line shuffled to a halt and a guard busied himself undoing Sunday's shackles. Puzzled, Sunday looked around. The man with the whip was talking to a smartly dressed Confederate officer.

"Dumb as a post," he said, indicating Sunday with a dismissive wave. "He'd be perfect. If the prisoners can't talk to him, they sure as hell can't bribe him."

The officer nodded slowly. "Good enough. Him and the simple boy'll do. Put him in the cart."

Sunday found himself in one of the carts that had just discharged its load of lumber. The other slave ignored Sunday, either staring vacantly at the wagon deck or looking around as if seeing the world for the first time.

The wagon rumbled uncomfortably through Richmond's streets toward the river. At length they turned onto Carey Street and stopped in front of a three-story brick building. Armed guards patrolled the front, and pale faces stared out of the barred windows. From one corner, a dilapidated wooden sign swayed disconsolately in the breeze. "L. Libby & Sons, Ship Chandlers and Grocers."

Sunday assumed they were to be put to work in this warehouse — so many armed guards suggested that it stored something very valuable. But why all the faces in the windows?

Sunday and his companion were roughly bundled out of the wagon and to a wooden shack behind a large stone building across about fifty feet of open ground from the warehouse. The dirt floor of the single room was covered with straw. A sagging cot and battered table stood to one side of an old iron stove. A gray-haired black man sitting on the cot looked up as Sunday was shoved through the door.

"Got company fer you, Mathias," the guard said. "You boys git yourselves acquainted, then hot foot it over to the office and collect yer duties."

The two new arrivals stood awkwardly in the doorway as the old man examined them. "Well," he said at length, "you'd best come in, though I don't take much to company. What are your names?"

Sunday's companion gazed at his feet and stuttered painfully, "M-M-M-Moses."

"Well, Moses, looks like you spent too much time in the wilderness, but as long as you kin work, you'll do just fine. An' what would your partner's name be?"

Sunday opened his mouth to show his mutilated tongue.

"Good God Almighty," Mathias said. "You must've done somethin' powerful bad. Kin you write yer name?"

Sunday nodded, crouched down and scratched his name in the dirt floor.

"Sunday. Well, we got a fine Bible group here. Now, here are the rules. First, this is my place and I ain't too happy 'bout sharin' with you boys. I kind o' got used to bein' on ma own. So don't be botherin' me with any nonsense. You'll do your work an' keep to yourselves. And there's plenty o' work. They got more'n a thousand prisoners in Libby Prison yonder — not that we have much to do with them, 'cept carry out the bodies in the mornin'.

"Most o' our work is keepin' the offices clean, helpin' out at the hospital and off-loading supplies. It's hard, but I reckon you know about hard, and we ain't the only ones havin' it hard here. You can take comfort from this bein' one o' the few places in this great Confederacy where black folks live better than white, even if the white is Yankee."

Sunday caught a movement out of the corner of his eye. A large brown rat emerged from the straw, scuttled across the room and disappeared.

Mathias let out a dry laugh. "No, we ain't alone. Reckon there'll be more o' them fellas than prisoners across the way. But don't go a worryin'. You don't bother them and they'll not bother you, less'n they's particular hungry. Then they might just take to gnawin' on yer toes while you sleep. But I reckon the rats in this place eats better than the humans.

"You boys bother me as little as the rats do an' we'll get on just fine. I ain't looking fer conversation and, by the looks o' things, I ain't going to get much from a dummy an' a simpleton. Now, we'd best git on over there afore we's missed. You can pick up blankets from the storeroom when the work's done.

"An' a couple other things — they're be no talkin' to the prisoners — that'll git you a whippin' — and no selling or exchanging food — that'll git you shot. Simple enough?"

Sunday and Moses nodded.

"Good."

Mathias led the pair to the side of the prison that fronted a dirt street and a canal where, Sunday assumed, goods had been loaded and off-loaded before the war. The land sloped toward the canal, so the cellar was at ground level making it a four-story building on this side.

"That bottom floor — ain't no one allowed in there 'cept to get supplies and to put prisoners in the condemned cells. Can't get to it from inside, the doors and stairs are boarded over. Only way in is through that door there in the middle.

"Floor above's the offices we clean, the prisoners' kitchen and the hospital. Ain't no need fer you to go anywhere but that floor, 'less you're loadin' or unloadin' supplies. The top floor's only fer the prisoners."

As Mathias explained the setup, the odd trio traveled completely around the building and entered a door off Carey Street. Sunday found himself in a large room, fully a third of the length of the building and occupying the entire width. The ceiling was rough beams, and two rows of pillars divided the space. Three areas had been set off as offices.

One was so cluttered it was nearly impossible to see

the desk for the mountain of paper. More paper lay in stacks on the floor and on a long table set along one wall. Behind the desk, hunched over a document and with a large quill in his hand, sat a well-dressed round-faced man sporting a sweeping handlebar mustache.

"Erastus Ross," Mathias whispered as he led the other two over to a collection of buckets and mops. "He's the prison clerk."

The desk in the area beside Ross's was almost bare. On the wall behind it was a rack of hooks from which dangled an impressive assortment of large iron keys. Beside it was a gun rack holding a dozen muskets. The man at the desk looked older than Ross and his thin face sported a long, full beard. His sharp blue eyes followed Sunday's every move.

"Richard Turner," Mathias said as he bent to pick up a bucket. "He's the jailer. Now pick up a mop and bucket."

The third desk sat in a large corner area. The two walls had been whitewashed and sported several pictures of a woman and two children in fancy clothes, an engraving of a large house in a country setting and a photograph of a building that Sunday recognized as the one he was in now. Three cabinets and a small table were arranged neatly against one of the walls, and the desk sat beneath a large window, its papers in neat piles. The man at the desk was writing a letter, and Sunday could not see much of his face other than he was clean-shaven and had a full head of black hair. A soldier stood at rigid attention to his left.

"That's the commander, Major Winslow Blake," Mathias said under his breath. "Watch yerself. He's a sly one."

Loaded with buckets and mops, Mathias led the way to Blake's desk and the three stood, looking respectfully at their shoes. The commander ignored them as he put the finishing touches to his letter. Then he blotted the ink dry, folded it and handed it to the soldier.

"See that this gets delivered promptly."

The soldier saluted crisply and retreated.

"Permission to clean the commander's office?" Mathias asked.

"So these are the new blacks," Blake said, ignoring the question. "Good. I shall now expect three times as much work. Carry on."

Blake went back to his paperwork, and Sunday, Moses and Mathias began scrubbing and mopping the floor.

Sunday was happy. The work didn't seem hard but, even better, they were barely guarded at all. Escape should be easy.

W A L T

August 23, 1863
Libby Prison
Richmond, Virginia

Walt shuffled to a stop in the dusty street in front of the imposing prison building, tired and thirsty after the long walk from the train station. He was also bruised on the back from a rock thrown from the shouting crowd that had followed the prisoners through the streets.

The journey had not been particularly difficult, but it had been long. Short stretches packed into railway cattle cars or goods wagons had been interspersed with marching or sitting around waiting. Food, when there was any, was poor, and everywhere, the local populace had come out to stare and hurl abuse and, occasionally, more solid objects.

But what had hurt more than any of the stones had been Nate's silence after their first meeting. Walt had tried to talk with his cousin several times but had been rebuffed by curses or a sullen silence. This wasn't the Nate he had known and he couldn't see what he had done to deserve the reaction. Now he supposed they would be separated again, probably forever, and he would never understand.

Walt looked disconsolately up at the red brick building with its thickly barred windows and armed guards. At least it meant an end to traveling, he thought bleakly. He hoped it also meant an end to Corporal Jake Stone. The man made Walt intensely uncomfortable. He had expected brutality and threats but not kindness.

Stone had treated Captain Fleming particularly harshly. As the senior officer in the group, Fleming was the one who spoke up for the prisoners. Walt, with the officers under false pretenses, had kept as invisible as possible. But Jake had seemed to go out of his way to be nice to him, slipping him extra scraps of food and keeping him at the front of the line, where he didn't have to breathe in the choking dust kicked up by the other prisoners.

Jake had even tried to engage Walt in conversation, quizzing him about Canada and suggesting that he might like to settle there after the war. Walt found it difficult to imagine that Jake was being kind to him just because he was Canadian, but he could think of no other reason.

The oddest incident had occurred on the train the day before. Jake had escorted Walt to the door of the goods wagon so that he could relieve himself. As Walt watched the countryside roll by, Jake had leaned un-comfortably close and said, "You wanna go home?"

"Of course."

"Maybe I kin help."

"Why would you do that?"

"I kinda took a likin' to your country when I was up there with Frank. There ain't gonna be too much left here after this war's done and I aim to move on. I reckon Canada'd be the place to go."

"Why do you need me? Why don't you just disappear one night? We couldn't stop you," Walt challenged.

"I got two reasons. One, the army looks none too kindly on deserting soldiers that it finds wandering the country. Richmond's a much easier place to git lost in.

"Two, it ain't near as easy to cross the border as it used to be. There's patrols all over. If'n I was traveling with a genuine Canadian goin' home, there'd be no problems. I'll make it worth your while," Jake added with a sly smile. "Now, 'nough of your questions. Do you want my help or not?"

Walt thought long and hard. He wanted desperately to go home. The lynched black man still haunted him. The war was too complex. He wanted the simple life of the farm. And he certainly had no desire to languish in a Confederate prison for the rest of the war. But could he trust Jake? He doubted it very much.

Jake Stone didn't seem to be as evil as Frank King, but Walt couldn't shake the memory of the pair kidnapping him from his farm. He could still see the flames leap from the byre and hear the screams of the trapped cow within. The cow, McKenzie, had been almost a pet, and King and Stone had deliberately set the fire. It was not a memory that inspired trust. Besides, would Walt be doing something that would drag Canada into this war? Might he harm his father? And what would happen to Walt when Jake didn't need him anymore?

Walt would take his chances at Libby.

"I've seen what your and Frank King's schemes lead to and I want no part of this one," Walt said at last. "I'll manage on my own."

"You're making a big mistake," Jake hissed in Walt's ear. "I know you ain't no real officer. One word from me and you'll end up with the other scum in Andersonville or Belle Isle and, believe me, you don't want to go to either o' them places. You think on what I'm saying now."

Walt looked up at the scores of white faces staring out of the upper windows. In one window an arm waved.

"Welcome to Rat Hell, boys!" a voice shouted. "We're sure glad to see you. It's getting a might lonely here."

"Shut up, Yankee," a guard responded.

"Now, that ain't nice. I was just welcoming our new friends into the bosom of the family. There's no need to —"

A musket crashed, a puff of brick dust sprouted beside the window and the face disappeared.

"That's enough sport for now."

Walt lowered his gaze to see an officer striding toward them. The man was immaculately dressed and clean-shaven. His black hair was perfectly parted and slicked down. There was a smile on his round, boyish face, but something in his expression sent a shiver down Walt's spine. That's how a snake looks the instant before it strikes, he thought.

Jake saluted. The officer ignored him and addressed the prisoners. "Who's the senior officer here?"

Captain Fleming took as much of a step forward as his shackles would allow. "I believe I am, sir. Captain Henry Fleming, 17th New York Regiment. At your service."

The Confederate officer looked long and hard at Fleming. "At my service indeed, Captain. I admit it has been ten long years, but do you not remember me, Henry?"

Fleming's brow furrowed in concentration. "Winslow? Winslow Blake?"

"The very same. Cadet Winslow Blake, West Point class of fifty-three. Seventeenth in the class to your tenth, I believe. Now a mighty major in the army of the Confederate States of America and commander of Libby Prison. We chose different sides."

Fleming nodded slowly. "It seems so."

"And it also seems that I am the jailer and you are a prisoner in this godforsaken place. I cannot guarantee that your stay will be short or comfortable, but if you behave and keep your men in line, you may survive. Do you undertake to do so?"

"I cannot, Winslow. I am a soldier. It is my duty to escape and cause as much difficulty for the enemy as I can."

"Stubborn as ever. Well, be warned. Comrades we may have been at the Point, but that was long ago. You will be treated just as the others. If you try to escape, I shall see you shot. And it is 'Major Blake' when you address me. Is that understood?"

"Yes, sir," Fleming snapped back formally.

Blake beckoned over a guard. "Take these men in and untie them. Register their names with Mr. Ross and put them in Streight's Room — there have been enough deaths of late to make space. And you, corporal." Blake turned his reptilian gaze on Jake. "Take your comrade and report to the duty sergeant on the main floor. He will show you to your quarters."

"But, sir," Jake began. "Our unit is —"

"Do not question me," Blake said coldly. "Your unit will not miss you. No one sends their best men to escort prisoners. The dregs is the best I can expect for this work. Besides, it is simple mathematics. You bring me more prisoners, I need more guards. Many of the prisoners are honorable men whom I would be happy to call my friends under different circumstances. Yet I will not hesitate to have troublemakers shot. That holds doubly true for the rabble that police this place. Now, go and report."

For a split second, Walt thought Jake was going to argue, but he controlled himself, mumbled a "Yes, sir" and strode toward the building. Nate slouched after him, and Walt and the others shuffled along behind.

Inside, the rope around the prisoners' ankles was removed, they were searched, and any pitiful valuables they had managed to hold on to were removed. Then they were led, one by one, to a cluttered desk and ordered to give their names.

"Give your name as Lieutenant Andrew Davis," Fleming whispered as he and Walt awaited their turns.

"Why?" Walt asked.

"If there is to be an exchange of prisoners, as there is from time to time, they will check the officers lists and find poor Andrew's name. It will do Andrew no harm and it might get you home sooner."

After all their names were entered by Ross's flowery script in his leather-bound book, the prisoners were led up two flights of stairs and shoved into a large, crowded room.

The room was as wide as the building and a hundred feet long, subdivided by two rows of sturdy wooden pillars. Numerous barred, glassless windows stretched almost the full seven feet from floor to ceiling on three sides. The floor was bare boards, where it wasn't covered with horse blankets and lying or sitting men. An iron stove and water trough were the only furniture.

As close as Walt could guess, there were nearly two hundred officers in the room, looking like a collection of tramps in fragments of uniform and items of civilian clothing. After his time in the army, Walt was used to unpleasant smells, but the heavy odor rising from the confined, unwashed bodies made him glad of the open windows.

The newcomers were greeted with grunts and low curses. Only one man, tall and heavy-set, stepped forward to welcome them. His hairline was receding, but a profuse beard grew along his chin, leaving his ready smile clearly visible.

"Colonel Abel D. Streight," he said, extending a hand to Fleming. Streight was dressed marginally better than the others, in the tattered remnants of a military jacket. "Welcome to our humble home. I fear I cannot offer you much in the way of hospitality, other than the comfort of being amongst your comrades in arms instead of the perfidious Confederates.

"The rules are simple here. Do as you are told, do not shout insults at the guards outside, stand to be counted twice a day, and answer the roll when it is called. The iron stove provides heat when we have wood and the trough provides water for washing. As for the latter, I recommend being quick after the water is changed or remaining comfortable with your dirt. Buckets are provided for night activities and are emptied every morning.

"As to the prison, there are nine rooms, six on these top two floors for our luxurious accommodation. On the main floor, there is the commander's room, which you will already have become acquainted with; a kitchen and dining area for prisoners' use and a hospital that you would do well to avoid at all costs. There is no access to the basement, which contains storerooms, a carpentry shop and some private cells that you would also do well to avoid.

"Now, I suggest that you seek out some patches of floor to call your own and lay out what blankets you may have. Come the winds of fall, you will be glad of them. Do you have any questions?"

"How does one escape?" Fleming asked.

Streight looked at him long and hard. "Are you

acquainted with the tale of the lion and the fox?"

Fleming shook his head.

"The one where the animals' footprints led into the lion's den?" Walt asked.

"Indeed." Streight ran a friendly eye over Walt. "You appear mighty young to be a full lieutenant," he mused. "But no matter. The lion, king of the jungle, invited all the animals to call upon him and pay their respects. The animals were flattered, so they made their way to his den. Only the wily old fox delayed. At length, he approached the den and studied the tracks. All led into the den, but none came back out, so the fox decided not to pay his respects to the king.

"Libby is like the lion's den. All tracks lead in and none out. Which is not entirely true. There are three ways out. The most common is through the hospital and out in a wooden box.

"The second way is to be exchanged for Confederate prisoners back home. Unfortunately, there have been no exchanges for months now. The Confederates seem to place too high a value on us to lose us for a few of their own."

"And the third way?" Fleming asked.

"The easiest of all," Streight said with a smile. "Stay alive until Lincoln wins the war. In the meantime, I suggest you get settled before evening count. Perhaps we can talk more later."

Feeling very out of place among so many officers, Walt followed Captain Fleming to a far corner.

"You have no blanket?" Fleming asked.

"No, sir."

"Well, you may share mine, it is large enough; although it does smell somewhat of horse. I suspect when the cold weather comes, we may be glad of each other's heat. And stop calling me sir. Remember, you are a fellow officer."

"Yes, s—"

SUNDAY AND NATE

August 24, 1863
Libby Prison
Richmond, Virginia

Sunday lifted the dead man under the arms while Moses took his feet. The body, little more than skin stretched over angular bones, was very light but it smelled vaguely unpleasant.

Carefully, the pair placed the corpse in the rough pine box, which they carried to the door. All around them, men almost as skeletal as the corpse lay on the filthy straw of the floor, lethargically watching their progress. A man in a stained apron moved among the patients, bending over each in turn, checking for a pulse if they were unconscious and exchanging a few words if they responded. There was little else he could offer.

This removal of bodies from the hospital each morning was the work Sunday liked least. But, with luck, he wouldn't have to do it for long. Several times in the past six days, Sunday could have walked away from the prison unchallenged. He hadn't because he needed a plan. A black man alone on Richmond's streets wouldn't last long, unless he had a good excuse or could stay out of sight. Since Sunday couldn't talk, the first option was impossible, and he would have to get to know Richmond's streets and alleys much better to hide in them. He would also need to know where the closest Union soldiers were encamped. He didn't want to retrace his long and painful escape from Nate's plantation along the Underground Railroad.

"Hurry along there," the man in the stained apron encouraged Sunday and Moses.

Sunday squinted against the harsh morning sunlight as he came out onto Carey Street, where Mathias waited with the cart.

"Only one this mornin'?" he asked as Sunday loaded the coffin. "Must have bin a good night. Now, Moses, you begin cleaning out the hospital. The doctor'll show you what to do. Understand?" Moses nodded disinterestedly.

"Good. Me an' Sunday here's goin' to the buryin' ground with this boy. Sunday needs to know the road so's he can do it if I get sick."

Sunday's heart leaped. Here was his chance to learn more about Richmond streets, and a future journey to the burying ground might offer escape. Sunday hauled himself up beside Mathias, as the old man flicked the reins. The equally old horse began its plodding journey.

"I've seen five or six boxes piled up in back some

mornins," Mathias told Sunday. "Worst in the winter. It's the cold that gets them. No flesh on their bones to keep 'em warm and no glass in the windows to keep out the wind. Why, I was treated better'n these boys when I was on the plantation."

Sunday tuned out. Mathias liked to talk but rarely wanted a reply, which made Sunday his ideal companion.

Sunday looked around as they moved away from the prison. On reflection, an evening break would probably be better than one this early in the morning — he would have the entire night before he was missed.

As the cart passed the guards' barracks, a soldier was heading toward the door. Sunday immediately forgot about escape. He could only stare. Was that Nate McGregor?

As the cart drew level, the soldier turned and froze in recognition. He half raised his hand in greeting before ducking in the doorway.

"… and I ain't sayin' them Yankees is good or nothin', but it ain't right that they're treated that bad," Mathias rambled on, oblivious to the drama.

Memories flooded Sunday's mind: Nate and he playing as boys, life on the plantation, the escape from Shiloh. It seemed as if he could never escape the past.

Nate collapsed on his cot in the guards' barracks across Carey Street from the prison. Had that been Sunday on the cart with the old black man? Even as he wondered, he knew it had been. Somehow, Sunday was here working at the prison. Last he'd heard from Walt, Sunday was joining a black regiment of the Union Army. So how had he got here?

Nate's sense of unreality at meeting Walt again was compounded. Why did fate keep thrusting his past at him?

During the endless tedium of the previous night's guard duty, walking back and forth along the prison wall, Nate had convinced himself that mindless repetition was exactly what he wanted. Walt was out of sight behind the thick wall and, with every trudging step, Nate had forced him out of mind as well. By the time Nate had dragged his exhausted body back to the guard room, he had almost convinced himself he was content. If he worked at it, he could build a wall as thick and high as the wall around Libby to keep out memories.

Then Sunday had looked down at him from a coffin wagon.

To keep from screaming in frustration, Nate stood and paced the length of the room. Cots lined both walls, muskets were propped in corners, and equipment hung from nails randomly pounded into the rough wooden walls. A handful of off-duty soldiers were sleeping or sitting on their cots talking quietly. The rest of the beds were empty.

Nate stopped beside the door. In a desperate effort

not to think, he read the notice pinned on the back of it, a list of rules and regulations.

1. There will be a roll call of prisoners at 7:30 a.m. and at 5 p.m. every day.
2. No prisoner will be allowed to leave quarters under any pretext whatsoever without special permission from the commanding officer.
3. No prisoner shall be fired upon by the guard unless in revolt or attempting escape.
4. Prisoners are not allowed any communication with persons outside the prison.
5. There is to be no conversation, intercourse or trading with the prisoners, in any manner whatsoever.
6. The guard off duty must remain constantly at the guardhouse ready for instant service and their guns must be kept on the rack.
7. The firing of one gun at night or two during the day will be the signal for immediate assembling of the guard.
8. These rules and regulations must be read to the new guard every morning before posting the first relief.

Nate took perverse pleasure in the rules. They meant he didn't have to think, and if he didn't think then he wouldn't care — would he?

The heavy door pushed inward and Nate had to step back sharply. Jake Stone stood in the doorway.

"Well, well. If it ain't the Yankee lover."

A couple of men nearby chuckled.

"I've fought in more battles against the Yankees than you," Nate said angrily. "I didn't spend my time as a low crimping agent, kidnapping boys to sell to raiders little better than outlaws."

Several men sat up, hoping for a fight.

"Why, you little —" Stone held himself in check when he saw the interest they were attracting. "We'd best have words outside, boy."

Nate couldn't back down in front of the other guards. He had no choice but to follow the big man out onto the street, even if it meant a fight. To his surprise, Stone was all smiles when he turned around.

"Didn't mean nothin' in there," he said in an oily voice. "Some o' them boys don't have your cultured background, an' I got to put on a bit of a show to keep 'em in line. You understand?"

Nate didn't but nodded.

"Good. I reckon we could become good friends."

"Why's that?" Nate asked, puzzled.

"'Cause we got an interest in common."

"I doubt that."

"What about that cousin o' yours?"

"What about him?"

"Him an' me go some ways back."

"To Frank King. I know all about that."

"Old Frank's long dead and gone. But he left me a present."

"A present."

"A gold sort of present. Problem is he left it up in Canada and it ain't so easy to go on up there these days — especially a lone deserter. I need help and your cousin Walt's the one as kin help me. I wasn't aimin' to be a guard in this hole. I was aimin' to skedaddle with your cousin soon as we reached Richmond, but now he's stuck inside them walls and I'm out here. You can help. There'd be a share of the gold fer both o' you."

"I don't want your gold," Nate said angrily.

"I don't reckon you want to see young Walt carried out o' Libby in a wood box neither."

Nate didn't want any contact with Walt, but he certainly didn't wish him harm. "Do you mean to help him escape?"

"Let's not be gettin' ahead of ourselves. Afore we talk about leavin', we need to talk to your cousin."

"But contact with prisoners is forbidden."

"That it is, but it goes on all the time. I reckon a smart boy like you can work out a safe way, especially if'n it means saving him from a wooden box. You just let me know when it's set up and I'll tell you what to say."

Jake went back into the guardhouse, leaving Nate standing on the dusty street. Walt, Sunday, escapes, mysterious gold — Nate wanted no part of any of them, but he was being drawn into something against his will. He could ignore Walt and Sunday, but not Stone. He could make Nate's life unbearable and would probably enjoy doing so.

Why wouldn't people leave him alone? But, Nate thought ruefully, he did have a way to contact Walt.

Cursing under his breath, he returned to the guard-house to get a few hours' sleep before the dead cart returned from the burial ground.

W A L T

September 15, 1863
Libby Prison
Richmond, Virginia

"Lieutenant Davis." The whispered words and the hand shaking his shoulder woke Walt from a deep, dreamless sleep. It took him a few moments to realize that Streight was addressing him. Streight put his finger to his lips. "Follow me."

Stepping carefully over the sleeping bodies, Walt followed Streight into the corridor and down the stairs to the inmates' kitchen on the ground floor. At the door, Streight knocked and gave a low whistle. The door opened and they were ushered in by Captain Fleming. Puzzled by the secrecy, Walt looked around the large room. The moonlight cast a silvery glow over the rough-hewn tables and the racks of pots and pans along the walls, giving everything a ghostly look. But it was the large iron cooking stove at the far end that caught

Walt's attention — it had been moved.

Normally, the stove stood in front of a brick fireplace almost large enough for a man to stand in. With it moved to one side, Walt could see that, where there should have been a solid wall of blackened bricks, there was a gaping hole.

"What's —?" he started to ask, turning to Fleming.

"Not yet," Streight replied. "Come on."

The trio crossed the room to the fireplace. In a smooth movement, Streight turned his back, ducked and stepped through the hole.

"You next," Fleming said to Walt. "It's only about an eight-foot drop. Let yourself down with the rope."

A lot more hesitantly than his predecessor, Walt backed through the hole, which sloped sharply before it opened out into another room, darker than the kitchen, but the moonlight was helped by several flickering tallow candles. The floor was covered with a thick layer of damp straw; its smell reminded Walt achingly of McKenzie's byre … when it had needed cleaning. A figure was crouched by the far wall, flapping his hat violently at something near the ground. As Walt looked around, several bright pairs of eyes glinted back at him.

"Don't mind the rats," Streight said. "They're more a nuisance than anything else. Although it's not particularly pleasant being in a confined space with them."

Fleming climbed through the hole to join them.

"This is the cellar room under the hospital," Streight explained. "We're relatively safe here, but we need to keep the noise down. The tunnel starts over there."

"Tunnel?" Walt asked.

"Yes. How did you think we were going to escape?"

"But you said there were only three ways —"

"I lied." Even in the dim light, Walt could see Streight's broad smile. "It is best if only a few know of our activities. When the time comes, more will know."

"And that time is not far off." Fleming smiled.

As they talked, the three moved across the floor, which felt oddly lumpy, until they were standing beside the crouched figure. Now Walt could see that he was hunched in front of a fair-sized hole in the cellar wall fanning air into the black space. A large rock, the size of the hole, stood to one side.

"Where does it go?" Walt asked.

"This is the outside wall at the east end of the building," Streight explained. "On the other side of it there is about fifty feet of open ground and then a shed that backs onto a warehouse. The shed is our goal."

"We're almost there," Fleming added, "although it is difficult to judge exactly because the tunnel has to wind around large rocks and we cannot get outside to measure."

"How long have you been working on this?" Walt could hardly believe that all this had been going on under the very noses of the prison guards.

"About six weeks," Streight replied, "but this is our third attempt. The first time, we tried to tunnel to a sewer line so we could escape into the river, but the ground was too wet — it collapsed. The second tunnel ran into the building's foundation logs. There was no way through or around them.

"This is our only option. It is a long tunnel, but the ground has been mostly good for digging.

"Two men work at a time, one digging and the other" — Streight indicated the man on the ground before him — "keeping the air circulating and dragging the dirt out. The string coming out of the hole is tied to the digger's ankle so we can communicate — two tugs means come out, three, a problem. When the digger has filled the spittoon — the only thing we could find to carry the dirt — he removes the string from his ankle and ties it around the spittoon. Then we can drag the dirt out. It's awkward — we need a double length of string so that the digger can pull the spittoon back in, and it's always getting tangled — but there is no other way."

"Where do you put the dirt?" Walt asked.

"Under the straw." Fleming pushed some straw aside with his foot to expose a pile of moist earth. That explained the lumpy floor.

"I'll help dig," Walt volunteered. He didn't like the idea of crawling into the hole — he had never been comfortable in small dark spaces — but this was the chance he had been looking for. If he helped with the digging, there was less chance of being left behind.

"Good," Streight said. "And you shall. We are always in need of strong diggers, but that is not why we brought you here. We need you to help in another way."

"I'll do what I can." Walt had no idea what he was getting into, but he meant what he said. The weeks of confinement in Libby had been a nightmare. He was filthy, lice-ridden and hungry, but none of that was as bad as the boredom. Walt spent hours dreaming of the woods and fields around Cornwall. He would give anything for an hour hunting rabbits or just walking through the trees.

"We need maps," Streight said. "We have been collecting civilian clothing for those who are going out, but we need to be able to get out of Richmond as quickly as possible. To do that, the escapees will need maps."

"I don't have any maps, and I don't know Richmond. This is the only time I've been here — and all I've seen is the inside of the prison."

"But you have a friend on the outside."

Nate! Walt had seen him on guard duty a couple of times, but he had never tried to contact him. The penalties — for both the prisoners and guards — were too severe.

"My cousin Nate. But how can I contact him?"

Streight handed Walt a note scrawled on a piece of creased paper.

"This was passed to a prisoner by one of the slaves. It was addressed to a Walt McGregor, but there was no one by that name here, so the soldier brought it to me. I showed it to Fleming and he told me your story. Don't worry, I won't turn you in."

Walt took the note and squinted to read it in the low light. It was actually two notes, one written above the other. The top one was from Nate.

September 12th, 1863

Walt,

I don't know if you know this, but Sunday is here at the prison as a slave. He has agreed to pass messages between us. He will write below how to do it.

I hope it is not too bad inside.

Nate

Walt's heart leaped. The note broke the silence Nate had imposed on the journey, but it said very little other than giving him the surprising news that Sunday was at Libby. Walt hurried on to the second note. It was much less formal.

Walt:

As Nate sed I am a slave here at the Libby prison and Mister Nate is a gard. Mister Nate cannot talk right to you, but I will take a letter to him if you want to rite one. If you put it at back of the flour bin in the kichen, then Moses — he is the idiot slave but he ain't as dumb as he makes out — will take the note when next he bring supplies up and will give it to me. Mathias don't like for me to come up to the kichen.

I hope your doing well and this reach you.

Your frend,
Sunday

"Who exactly is Sunday?" Streight asked.

"He used to be Nate's slave on the plantation near Charleston, but he ran away and came up to Canada. He stopped me from killing Nate at Shiloh. He was with the 54th Massachusetts but he must have been captured."

"You trust him?"

"With my life."

"And this cousin, Nate?"

"Of course."

Streight nodded thoughtfully. "All right, then. Write a letter back to Nate. Keep it simple, just say hello and complain a little about the life here. We need to establish that the line of communication is secure. Then, if he is willing, we can ask for maps. But we must hurry. We are due to break through soon and we need —"

"Three tugs — there's a problem." The man by the tunnel dropped his hat and hauled on the string.

With one last violent tug, a battered tin spittoon filled with dirt flew out and landed in the straw.

Scuffling noises in the tunnel were getting closer. A pair of sleek brown rats shot out of the hole and disappeared under the straw. The men watched nervously as a pair of filthy feet were thrust into the room. They were followed by the rest of a man, covered in mud and dressed only in shorts. He stood up and scraped the worst of the wet mud off his face. He was breathing heavily and obviously extremely agitated.

"That was close," he said. "I broke through."

"In the shed?" Streight and Fleming asked simultaneously.

"No. Short of the shed. I was digging up like you said, but we must have been shallower than we thought. A clod of dirt fell in and then I saw his boots."

"Boots?"

"The guard! He was right there. Almost fell in the hole. I thought I was dead for sure. I don't know how he could have missed me, especially in the moonlight. He heard something all right — looked around, but must have thought it was a rat. I froze. It felt longer than that damned charge through the cornfield at Antietam.

"He eventually left and I stuffed dirt and my shirt into the hole and skedaddled back here. I ain't going back in there tonight."

"That's okay. How short are we?"

"I can't say. I couldn't see nothin' but his boots and I wasn't about to climb out and look around."

"No, I guess not," Streight said, patting the distraught digger on the shoulder. "We're finished for the night. You two go get cleaned up and try to get some sleep. We'll close up down here."

The digger nodded and crossed the cellar to the rope, followed by the crouching man.

"Damnation!" Streight kicked at the straw. "I hate this guesswork. Who knows where the hell we are."

"No one," Fleming said, "but maybe Walt here could find out."

"Yes," Streight agreed. "We must have an accurate measure of the distance from this wall to the shed. Your cousin could help with that."

"He will." Walt sounded confident, but was unsure what he was committing Nate to.

"Good, but first we need to make sure our notes can move back and forth safely. Write the first one tonight and put it behind the flour bin at breakfast. Now, we'd best get back." Streight and Fleming moved the rock into place over the tunnel mouth.

"Maybe you would like a turn digging tomorrow?" Streight asked Walt as he grabbed the rope up to the fireplace.

"I would," Walt said. His voice was eager, but he wasn't sure about crawling into the rat-infested tunnel.

Fleming emptied the last of the dirt out of the spittoon, tidied it up by the tunnel mouth and joined Walt, extinguishing candles as he came. Then they all clambered into the kitchen, pulled up the rope, replaced the bricks in the fireplace and pushed the stove back. Finally, Streight produced a bag of soot and sprinkled a layer over the hearth. When he had finished, it looked as though nothing had been disturbed.

Walt was on his blanket as dawn painted the bricks orange. As soon as it was light enough, he took out a pencil stub and wrote Nate a letter.

NATE

September 15, 1863
Libby Prison
Richmond, Virginia

Nate almost dropped his musket at the sound. It had been unusual, a soft plop, like a loosely filled bag of cotton hitting a solid floor. Nate was used to the scuttling of rats, but this sounded different. It had also sounded very close, although Nate couldn't tell from which direction it had come. Clutching his musket tighter, he looked around.

The moonlight was bright, but the shadows were deep along the prison wall and by the shed at his back. Nothing was moving. Nate took a few tentative steps, stood for a couple of minutes, tilting his head trying to penetrate the silence, but there was nothing. Shrugging, he resumed his patrol. It must have been an animal and Nate had been startled because he was daydreaming so deeply.

Nate dreamed a lot these days, both awake and asleep. Guard duty was painfully boring, and he had nothing in common with the other guards, who tended to be a rough lot without the least interesting conversation. The only thing that kept Nate's mind occupied was the note he had written to Walt. Oddly, he found himself looking forward to a reply. Every time he saw Sunday, his spirits leaped in anticipation. At first his reaction had annoyed him — he wanted to feel isolated and protected in his cocoon of not caring — but he couldn't help it. When no reply came, Nate had to admit he was disappointed. He even wished he had been less curt in his note. Perhaps Walt was annoyed at his tone. Nate kicked the dry ground. It was becoming harder to keep his emotional walls from crumbling. They weren't nearly as solid as the walls around Walt after all.

Nate walked and thought until the sun was above the horizon and the noises of the awakening prison filtered through the bars. When he was relieved of duty, he got some beans and cornbread and ate them with a tin mug of scalding coffee. The other guards ignored him and Nate was happy enough that they did.

As the day took shape around him, the long hours of night duty began to tell. Nate yawned and stretched. If he was tired enough, he would sleep, the best way to kill a few hours. Nate seemed to need more sleep than the other guards, who spent their spare time gambling, swearing and trying to get passes to go into town to carouse. That was fine with Nate because that meant he often had the barrack room to himself.

That was the case when he returned to his cot and luxuriated in removing his boots and stowing his musket. Nate was nearly asleep when he heard a soft knock on the door. He ignored it but, when it was repeated, groggily opened the door.

Sunday looked extraordinarily guilty standing in the doorway. He shuffled from foot to foot and cast nervous glances over his shoulder.

"Sunday!" Nate exclaimed. In his half-asleep state, he couldn't imagine why Sunday was here. Before he could work it out, Sunday thrust a scrap of paper into Nate's hand and fled. The note was grubby and tightly folded, but the few lines of writing on the inside were neat and legible.

September 15th, 1863

Cousin Nate,

I hope this reaches you safely. I know you are still here because I see you occasionally on patrol.

Things are not too bad in here, although it is a bit crowded and the rats can be a nuisance. An extra room or two and a few cats would make a world of difference. I do miss the open farm spaces of Cornwall. We are allowed to write three lines of a letter each week and I have sent one to Father, but have not heard back yet.

I hope you are well and that we can get to know each other better when this is all over.

If this arrived safely, and you would like to reply, give a note to Sunday.

Best regards,
Walt

A tear plopped on the page. Nate rubbed his eyes angrily. This was ridiculous. What did he have to cry about? He had seen men dismembered by shells and not cried, yet a simple note from a relative he barely knew and who, not so long ago, he had wished had not existed, and he was blubbering like a baby. It made no sense — but he would give everything he had to have a life like Walt's to go back to. Rubbing his sleeve roughly across his face, Nate rummaged in his kit until he found a scrap of paper and his pencil. He began writing in small, tight script.

WALT

September 18, 1863
Libby Prison
Richmond, Virginia

Walt kicked back hard with his left foot. The rat squealed in pain and scuttled down the tunnel.

The hard digging in the cramped conditions, the total darkness when the candle went out, the terror of being buried alive — nothing was as repugnant as the scratchy feeling of the rats running over his bare legs and back. It sent shivers down his spine and always produced a violent involuntary reaction.

Walt crammed a last handful of dirt into the spittoon, untied the string from his ankle and secured it around the neck of the battered receptacle. He tugged on the string and watched it jerk its way back. Now he could rest for a few moments, if you could call lying almost naked in a dark, damp, rat-infested tunnel resting. But it was a relief that the digging was killing work. There was no room to crouch or kneel, so it was done either lying on his back with the dirt falling in his eyes or on his stomach working blindly above his head. Either way, Walt's arms had to be held up at an awkward angle, and they ached horribly.

His tools were a kitchen knife, a chisel stolen from the carpentry shop and his bare hands. A tallow candle flickered fitfully beside him. Its meager light was more a comfort than a help. Walt knew that as long as the flame burned, the man at the tunnel entrance was fanning enough oxygen for him to breathe.

This was Walt's third shift in the tunnel. He had learned that the most frightening time was not the actual work, but the simple act of putting his head into the black hole and beginning the crawl into what could be a tomb — the urge to stay back in the cellar was almost overwhelming. But once he was crawling, he was too busy to be frightened.

Walt had learned a lot, too, about earth. Every spittoonful had a different character. Some was damp and easy to dig but dangerous, as large pieces fell on him. At other times it seemed to take hours to dig a few inches through hard, clay-rich soil, but the walls remained smooth and safe. Then there were the rocks. Small ones could be dug out and pushed back out, but the large ones — and there had been four in the tunnel so far — had to be dug around.

A tug on the string tied to Walt's leg signaled that the spittoon was ready for its return journey. Walt reached back and began pulling on the string. He tried to fold it neatly so that it would unfold smoothly next time the spittoon had to be hauled out, but he always had to untie tangles at the end of each shift. Walt had no idea of time, but from the number of times he had sent the full spittoon back, he figured it must be approaching the end of his shift. Perhaps two or three more loads, then …

Walt felt a soft breath of air raise the hairs on the backs of his legs. The weak candle flame wavered and died, plunging him into total darkness. The string tied to the spittoon tightened and resisted Walt's pull. Somewhere behind Walt, the tunnel roof had caved in.

For a long moment, Walt had to concentrate on fighting down waves of panic. He tensed every muscle in his body to prevent his arms and legs from flailing about wildly and clenched his teeth to stifle the scream that rose in his throat. The words "buried alive" whirled around his mind. Walt gasped to drag air into his lungs.

"Stop!" Walt had to shout aloud to regain some control. "You are not suffocating. There is plenty of air for you to crawl back and dig your way out."

Gradually, coherent thought returned. Perhaps it wasn't a big cave-in. Maybe he could push his way through it. Besides, the man at the other end of the string would be crawling in to help. Odd, Walt thought. He may save my life and I don't even know his name.

Slowly, Walt pushed backward with his hands and elbows against the sides and floor of the tunnel. Inch by inch, he worked his way toward the opening. If he concentrated on moving and tried not to imagine a slow death down here, his heart slowed. The worst moment was when a huge rat scuttled up his bare legs and across his back before brushing its hairy body against his cheek.

Eventually, Walt's feet came up against a wall of dirt. He pushed. His feet sank into the soft earth, but not through. Trying not to think how long the cave-in was, Walt began digging. He couldn't fully turn around, but by lying on his side and curling his legs up, he could reach down and scrape earth from below his feet, up past his body and into the tunnel.

Every so often, Walt would straighten his legs in an effort to break through, but to no avail. The more dirt Walt shoveled past his head, the more he had the feeling that he was in a grave. The space he was in was becoming more and more restricted, the air more foul. Soon he was gasping in short, shallow gulps, struggling to keep panic at bay. He would never get through.

Should he start digging up? If it was a big cave-in, it might be shorter to dig to the surface. Time was running out. Lights began to flash behind Walt's eyes and his oxygen-starved muscles cramped. The harder he tried to work, the less he achieved.

Walt stopped digging. With less physical activity, he managed to regain a little breath, but what good was that? He would die a lonely death with the rats. The thought of the rodents gnawing his face and eyes — perhaps even before he was dead — motivated Walt to one last effort. It was then that he felt something grasp his ankle. If he had had the wind, Walt would have screamed. His fevered mind imagined the skeletal hand of some long-buried corpse claiming him for its own.

Instinctively, Walt kicked out. His foot encountered something hard. A muffled "Damn!" reached his ears. Rotting corpses didn't swear. Relief surged over Walt, then blackness.

Walt came to on the cellar floor. Streight was crouching over him. "Good morning," he said.

All Walt could manage was a confused grunt.

"You were lucky, lucky the cave-in wasn't too big and lucky Fleming was here to pull you out — although he got a good kick in the jaw for his trouble."

"I panicked," Walt said.

"We all would have. It's the tunnelers' nightmare. "Have a drink." Streight held a bottle of water to Walt's lips and he drank greedily.

Walt's head ached fiercely, but otherwise he didn't feel too bad. "How's the tunnel?"

"Not too damaged as far as we can tell. Odd as it may seem to you, it wasn't a big cave-in, certainly not big enough to leave a depression in the ground above, which would have been a disaster. We should get it cleared tonight, but it has shown us that we must work quickly. Too many things are going wrong, and sooner or later one will end in disaster. We need that information from your cousin."

"But we have only exchanged two notes. We don't know for sure that the system is secure."

"We can't afford to come up too soon again. And another cave-in could expose the tunnel on the surface. Can you write another note asking your cousin to help us?"

"Sure."

"And stress that speed is of the essence. Meanwhile, we will prepare what civilian clothes we have for the escapees."

"How many are going out?" Walt tensed. Would he be going?

"About twenty-five people have been involved with the tunnel, so probably about that number on the first night."

"The first night?"

"Yes. If twenty or thirty men, spread across all the rooms, go, we should be able to hide their disappearance at the head count the following day. That will give them time to get away from the city. Then we can send the same number the next night. Once we cannot camouflage the numbers, we will send as many as possible through the following night. The first group should have the best chance, though."

"Am I to go?" Walt asked, his heart in his throat.

Streight looked hard at Walt's eager face. "Eventually, yes."

Walt's heart sank at the word "eventually." "But —"

Streight held up his hand. "You're too valuable to send out right away. Your cousin is vital to our success. It will be useful to have a trustworthy contact on the outside. I won't forbid you to go on the first night, but I would ask you to stay. The more men we get out, the more it will hurt the Confederacy."

"All right," Walt said, giving in. "I'll stay and keep in touch with Nate."

"Good lad. Now let's get you upstairs and cleaned up. This adventure is just beginning."

NATE AND SUNDAY

September 18, 1863
Libby Prison
Richmond, Virginia

Nate let the crumpled paper slip from his hand — his happiness at receiving the letter turning to anger and confusion. Over the past few days, Nate's mood had brightened with the receipt of chatty notes from Walt. He had even begun thinking about a life after the war, perhaps in an idyllically imagined Cornwall.

But he had been tricked again — not by death this time, but by betrayal. All his cousin wanted was information to help prisoners escape. Nate was sick of the war and the dreams of the Confederacy, but that was a long way from helping the enemy. Walt was using him.

"Damnation!" Nate cursed under his breath.

Sunday looked curiously at him. He had found Nate sitting, his back against the barracks wall, enjoying the morning sunshine. No one else was around, so

Sunday had waited to see Nate's reaction to the note. He knew it was important because Walt had scrawled on the front "Please get this to Nate as soon as possible." Judging by Nate's reaction, it was not good news.

Sunday pulled out the scrap of paper and pencil stub he always kept in his pocket and wrote "Wat is rong?"

Nate laughed bitterly. "Spelling isn't your strong suit, is it, Sunday? Read this."

Sunday took the note and read. As he did so, Nate talked on, almost to himself.

"Walt wants me to do something that would help him but hurt the side I am fighting for. I don't know what to do. This war is turning the whole world upside down. Father and I were comfortable on the plantation and everything was simple. Now the plantation is gone, Father is dead, and my cousin is asking me to betray my country. I wish life were simple again."

Sunday shook his head violently. Didn't Nate know anything? Didn't he remember? Maybe people didn't change. Nate was his father's son and would always be a slave-driving plantation owner.

Angrily, Sunday threw the note down, ripped his shirt off and turned his back to Nate. The hard, knotted scars of innumerable whippings stood out pale against his skin. On his shoulder, the brand of Nate's father's initials stood out accusingly. He spun back and opened his mouth, forcing Nate to see the ugly stump of his mutilated tongue.

Nate sat silently, guilt washing over him. He had felt guilty before — over Judith Henry choosing to stay in her house and being killed by a Yankee shell; over his father dying ill and insane; and over Jeff dying amidst thousands at Gettysburg. That guilt, Nate saw now, was mere self-pitying misery about something he had no control over.

But this was different. His guilt stood in front of him, a living human being. Nate had not whipped or branded Sunday, nor cut out his tongue. Frank King had performed those terrible acts, but Nate's father had trusted King and given him the freedom to do them. Nate's father knew what was going on — he was responsible.

And so was Nate.

Nate had known slaves had been whipped and branded, but he had accepted it as normal. In the bigger world of war, individuals had to take responsibility for their actions. He hadn't done so on the plantation, but he could now. Was the Confederacy just a bigger version of his father's plantation? It was his country and he loved it, but its ugly implications were on Sunday's body.

Sunday stood glaring down at Nate.

"I'm sorry," Nate said.

A puzzled expression crossed Sunday's face. What was Nate sorry for? Nate couldn't even begin to explain. Instead he said, "Come back this afternoon, Sunday. I want to write a note to Walt."

Still confused, Sunday nodded and retreated to the slave shack. Nate went into the guardhouse and found a pencil and paper. Neither saw Walt's note lying forgotten in the dust — or Jake Stone hovering nearby.

SUNDAY

September 18, 1863
Libby Prison
Richmond, Virginia

Sunday was terrified. The footsteps were getting closer.

Nate had given him the note for Walt late in the afternoon, but he'd had no excuse to go to the prisoners' kitchen and Jake Stone had kept him busy with the stores and scrubbing out the hospital. Nate had said the message was urgent, so Sunday had risked sneaking in after dark. Now he was hiding beside the flour bin as footsteps came down the corridor.

The kitchen door opened and three figures, shielding flickering candles, entered and moved across to the fireplace. Sunday held his breath.

"I'll check for a note."

Sunday exhaled loudly as he recognized Walt's voice.

"Who's there?" Walt said. The other two figures froze. Sunday stood and began signing his name.

"Sunday?"

Sunday stepped forward and handed Walt the note. As he squinted at it, the other two men gathered around, looking suspiciously at Sunday.

"He'll do it," Walt said. "Nate will pace out the distance tonight and try to find the most direct route out of town tomorrow. But, Sunday, why are you hiding here?"

Sunday rapidly signed the story of why he had not been able to get the note placed earlier.

"What's he doing?" Streight asked.

"He's signing. He has no tongue, so he speaks with this hands."

"And you understand this?"

"Yes."

"Can you speak it as well?"

"Of course. I learned with Sunday at home before we came down here. But that's not important now. Sunday says he couldn't get up here today, so he had to sneak in after dark. That's too dangerous. If he gets caught —"

"And too uncertain," Fleming interrupted. "The information is crucial now. If we don't get it in time or if it is interrupted, that could ruin the whole plan. We have to find a better way than notes behind the flour bin."

"We have a better way," Streight said. The others looked at him with puzzled expressions. "Fleming, did you know what was going on here with these hands fluttering around all over the place?"

"No, of course not."

"That's just it. I'll warrant not one man in a thousand can recognize that hand language, especially coming from a slave. As long as this boy — what's his name?"

"Sunday," Walt said eagerly, beginning to see what Streight was getting at.

"As long as Sunday doesn't obviously sign at someone right in front of him, everyone will assume that he is a little weak in the head and plays with his hands."

"So," Walt went on, "Sunday could pass messages to us with his hands and no one would know what he is doing."

"Exactly. He could stand in the middle of the street and tell us precisely how far we still have to dig. No one would be any the wiser."

The four men stood in silence, absorbing the implications of what Streight had said. They didn't need notes — Walt and Sunday could simply talk as they always had done.

"Will you do it?" Walt asked.

Sunday nodded and signed yes.

"All right." Streight was all business. "Now we need to organize a time and place where Sunday can sign and Walt can see him and reply if necessary. Meanwhile, Walt needs to write one last note to Nate telling him about the change. I'm going to enjoy the digging tonight."

WALT

September 19, 1863
Libby Prison
Richmond, Virginia

Walt leaned casually on the south-facing window ledge of the kitchen. The fall sun was warming away the chill in the early morning air. Across the street, a barge was making its way slowly along the canal, pulled by a mule. The driver was having a difficult time making the beast do what he wanted. Instead of a steady, plodding pull along the towpath, the mule kept on pulling away from the water, threatening to drive the barge against the side. Every time, the driver would let out a volley of curses and beat the mule with a long stick. Reluctantly, the mule would straighten out for a few yards before lurching once more to the side. Numerous men were at the windows enjoying the show.

"Proves how badly the Confederacy is doing." Streight stood at Walt's shoulder, drawing thoughtfully on his pipe.

"What do you mean?"

"Mules are not what you want for that work. They're too cantankerous and independent. Horses are much better. Every bargeman knows that. No doubt our friend down there knows and isn't too happy with his situation."

"Why does he use a mule, then?"

"I suspect he has no choice. Horses are also better for pulling gun carriages — and for cavalry charges. I'll bet his horse has been requisitioned by the army. Things must be desperate if they are requisitioning barge horses."

A gale of laughter swept through the soldiers at the windows as the mule lurched, almost pushing the driver into the water. Even the Confederate guards were engrossed by the comedy.

"But you used mules on your raid," Walt pointed out. "Everyone has heard of the Lightning Mule Brigade. It's famous."

"Famous it may be." Streight laughed. "And mules there certainly were, but 'lightning'? That term must be a joke."

"Why did you use mules if they are so difficult?"

"We had no more choice than the bargeman. We needed to move two thousand infantrymen right across Alabama to cut the railway lines at Rome, Georgia. Those men couldn't have stayed on a cavalry mount for half an hour. And a good cavalry horse needs a lot of caring for. Mules are easier for men who are used to marching. And we knew the terrain. Most of my men came from northern Alabama. We —"

"Alabama? But Alabama's Confederate."

"Just because a state legislature votes for secession doesn't mean that every citizen agrees. Not everyone in the South is a rich slave owner. My men were small farmers from the mountains. They never owned slaves and had nothing to gain from secession. You would be surprised how many men trickled over to the Union side. Why, I hear even some Canadians are involved."

Streight grinned at Walt. "Be that as it may, we did well with the mules, even though they were terrible, unbroken beasts. Once, they took to braying so loudly they alerted some nearby Confederate cavalry, who drove off four hundred of the beasts. I would have been glad to see them go except it meant that that many of our men had to walk.

"The only reason we covered as much ground as we did was that we never stopped, day or night. That's the other thing about mules — they are hardy beasts and will go on long after a horse would be broken down.

"But it didn't work." Streight gazed wistfully into the distance. "There were just too many cavalry, and when they got between us and Rome we had to fight. We had close to sixteen hundred men, tired but willing. They had only about five hundred, but they moved them about so cleverly that it looked as if we were outnumbered. Surrender seemed the only option, so I did.

"If I had known I was up against only five hundred I would have fought it out, but —"

"Here he comes!" Walt interrupted excitedly.

The supply wagon rumbled around the corner and stopped at the cellar door immediately below the window. Sunday and another slave jumped down and began unloading sacks of cornmeal. The plan was going to work — the nearest guards were distracted by the mule and barge. Then Walt's heart sank. A large figure sporting a thick black beard sauntered around the corner and stood watching the unloading. Did Jake Stone know about sign language?

Walt struggled to remember if he or Sunday had ever used it in front of Jake, but he couldn't remember. He was about to say something to Streight when Sunday's companion came back into view. He was prancing and gamboling about like an idiot, waving his arms wildly. Sunday was following him, trying to get him back to work. Jake watched dispassionately.

Sunday followed the other man, mimicking his movements. A few guards were beginning to pay attention to this new sport.

"What's going on?" Streight asked. "He shouldn't be attracting attention like that. He'll ruin the whole thing."

"No, he won't," Walt said. He was watching Sunday intently. The pair were dancing around madly now, and both the guards and the prisoners at the windows were laughing and shouting encouragement.

Sunday's companion was waving his arms randomly, but Sunday was not. Mixed in with the wildness were signs that Walt recognized — Sunday was talking to him.

Walt concentrated. There was his name sign, and a number, fifty, another number, three, and now a word, spelled out in bits and pieces, p–a–s–e–s. Walt laughed out loud.

"Why are you laughing?" Streight barked. "This is a disaster."

"No it's not," Walt said. "It's fifty-three paces to the shed, and I am laughing because Sunday never could spell."

Streight stared at Walt, then turned to look at Sunday. He had to laugh, too. "Clever boy," he said.

Eventually, amid a chorus of good-natured boos and shouts of "Shame!" Jake got the two slaves under control and back unloading the supplies. In the midst of all the shouting and gesticulating out the windows, Walt made the sign for "Okay" several times. He was sure Sunday glanced his way. Then Streight tapped him on the shoulder and the two retreated upstairs, where they told Fleming the news.

"Fifty-three paces," Fleming said. "We must be almost under it. We'll measure exactly tonight, but it can't be more than a few feet — only a night or two."

"He said something else as well." Walt grinned. "He signed 'Ravine northeast.'"

"The way out of town." Streight was obviously impressed. "Then Tuesday it is."

"Tuesday?" Walt asked.

"That's when we go through the tunnel. September 22, the anniversary of Lincoln's Emancipation Proclamation. We plan to have a party — good cover for the first escape group. The escapees will take clothes with them, change in the shed and casually stroll out into the street one or two at a time. There are only two possible problems."

"And Nate can help solve them." Walt could see where the conversation was going.

"He must," Streight said. "We don't know how the inside door from the shed to the building fronting the street is locked. If it is on the building side, getting to the shed only changes our prison."

"I can ask Nate."

"Excellent. The other thing is that the guard on this side will have a clear view of the street door we will be going out. Even if only one or two go at a time, it will look suspicious after a while."

"Not if the guard is Nate," Walt replied. "I will get a message to him about both those concerns."

"But be careful how you do it. You will have to give him details of our plan and the timing, so the message cannot fall into the wrong hands."

"It won't."

"Good," Streight said. "I'll begin organizing those who are going out."

Fleming and Walt sat silently as Streight threaded his way through the room, stopping to talk quietly with the men who were part of the plan.

"Are you going in the first group?" Walt asked.

"Yes," Fleming replied. "My name is on the list."

"Do you think the plan will work?"

"There is always the chance that something un-expected will happen, but —"

"No, I mean covering up the escapes so we can keep sending men out for several nights."

"That's more difficult," Fleming said thoughtfully.

"The longer the escape takes, the greater the chance that something will go wrong, and a lot of people are going to have to know about it. The head counts shouldn't be a problem. Streight has organized a system of moving men from room to room so there will always seem to be enough prisoners in any room. The problem is that, if the guards get suspicious, they will do a roll call by name — then we'll be sunk. The first batch should be well clear of the city by then, though."

"Are you going back to the army?"

"Of course. I'm an officer — I have an obligation. Besides, we have to win this war. But you — you're not an officer, not even an American."

"I don't know. When the war broke out, I wished Canada would get involved so I could fight for a simple cause — my country. Then when I was kidnapped to fight for the wrong side, all I could think of was escaping. After Shiloh, when Sunday and I were traveling north, it all seemed simple again — join the right side and fight against slavery, but now I am not so sure."

"Why is that?"

Walt thought back over the past two months. "I saw a man killed."

"But you must have seen many men die — at Shiloh, when the train was attacked —"

"Yes, but this was on the streets of New York."

"During the riots?"

"Yes. Do you remember the black man who had been lynched when you broke up the mob? It's him I keep thinking of. He wasn't a soldier. And the people who killed him — tortured him — were citizens of the town he lived in. They were supposed to be fighting on the same side, but they killed him in a more brutal way than any death I have seen on the battlefield. If I go back to the army, I will be fighting for those thugs as well as the good people. I would see that man's body swinging above the fire every time I went into battle. I don't know if I can do it."

"Thinking too much is not a good characteristic in a soldier."

"No, I suppose not. My father tried to tell me that the world was a complicated place — now I understand what he meant. The simple life of the farm looks good right now. At least I'd get something other than cornbread to eat." Walt shook off the gloom that had descended on him. "And Canadian rats are much friendlier than these secessionist ones."

Fleming laughed. "Well, right now it is simple — we have to get out of that hole and put a lot of miles between this place and ourselves."

Fleming moved away and Walt lay back, his mind filled with images of home, his father, the farm, Montreal. Even things that no longer existed: the comfort of talking to McKenzie in her byre, hunting rabbits with Touss. The ache of homesickness overwhelmed him. If only he could talk to his father.

But Fleming was right. For the moment, all that mattered was the breakout. Rousing himself, Walt carefully examined and rewrapped the bundle of clothes he had been collecting for his escape — if he got the chance.

SUNDAY

September 20, 1863
Richmond, Virginia

Sunday luxuriated in the only free time he had in the week. He had never been much of a churchgoer, although he enjoyed the singing, but a local temperance group had persuaded the authorities that a slave's soul was worth saving: they should be allowed to go to church. Not the same church as the white people, but that was okay with Sunday. Church was a pleasant break, and the small wooden building reminded him of the rough church at Shiloh where he had promised to say a prayer for his friend Touss.

He thought of another dead hero, too. Sunday had not known Colonel Robert Shaw well — they lived in different worlds. Shaw had lived in the sumptuous company of some of the great intellectuals of his day. Sunday had found these people daunting, even though they were unfailingly friendly to him. They spoke a language he didn't know and thought about things he could never understand.

Nevertheless, Sunday had admired Shaw and was indebted to him. He had created the 54th Massachusetts Regiment from nothing and had fought to get his black soldiers equal pay and decent weapons. Touss would have approved — black and white fighting together to achieve something worthwhile.

But the image of Shaw's bloodstained, limp body sliding into the mass grave at Fort Wagner haunted Sunday. Oddly, it produced no desire for revenge, just filled him with disgust at the squandering of thousands of good men like Shaw.

Sunday was sickened by the war. It was not a glorious crusade — it was Nate's hopeless charge across the field at Shiloh and his own along the beach at Fort Wagner. What had either achieved except grieving and pits full of bodies? Sunday wasn't sure he could go through that again.

But that was a matter for the future. Much more immediate were Walt and Nate. Sunday had read all the notes he'd carried, and Nate had explained a lot when he asked Sunday to pass messages by signs. Walt and the others were going to try to break out of the prison on Tuesday night. Walt had asked Nate if he could be on guard that night and if he could check the door inside the shed. Nate had agreed to both, but had looked so worried Sunday had said he would attend to the shed door. No one paid any attention to the slaves at night.

Nate had been grateful, but the idea had planted a seed in Sunday's brain — if he could get into the shed, what was to stop him from waiting for Walt and joining in the escape? Having a black man traveling with him would make Walt much less suspicious if anyone was looking for escaped prisoners.

The more he thought about it, the more Sunday liked the idea. The only questions were whether Walt would be among the escapees and whether Nate would join them.

Sunday found himself smiling broadly at the thought of a peaceful existence on Touss's old farm with Walt and Nate as neighbors.

Mathias, standing beside Sunday, took the smile for religious zeal and thundered out the hymn. Sunday nodded in time to the music, keeping his thoughts to himself.

WALT

September 22, 1863
Libby Prison
Richmond, Virginia

The celebrating in the prisoners' dining area was in full swing. The air was filled with a cacophony of drums, harmonicas and mouth harps. Feet thumped loudly on the floor and a wild assortment of voices rose in song. For overcrowded prisoners on a starvation diet, everyone appeared extraordinarily happy. The reason for such happiness was more immediate than the anniversary of Emancipation. At the far end of the room, men were disappearing behind the kitchen stove.

Streight and Walt stood by the stove helping the escapees on their way. Streight gave them final words of advice. "Wait in the shed or in the warehouse until the group before you has got clear. Don't leave more than three at a time. Get directions from Fleming in the cellar."

"Don't need no instructions," a cheerful, skinny lieutenant said. "Spent four years here afore the war. I know this old town like the back of my hand."

"Good. Then you will lead your party at least until you get into the countryside. Where do you aim on heading?"

"Williamsburg. That's the closest Union men. I figure on heading northeast, out by the old Fair Oaks battlefield, crossing the Chickahominy River above New Bridge, crossing the Yorkville Railroad and heading on down the Williamsburg Pike till I hear the ole 'Battle Hymn of the Republic' drowning out 'Dixie.' Shouldn't take more'n a handful of days, I reckon."

"Sounds like a good plan. Good luck."

Walt was caught up in the excitement yet tortured by not being able to go. Something told him this would be the only chance. He let his eyes drift over to the wild party. Far too many people knew — there was no way this could be kept the orderly night-by-night escape Streight had imagined. He was about to say something when Streight spoke first.

"How many is that?"

"I've counted twelve."

"About half. We should hold back until they start to come out. The men at the windows upstairs will let us know when the first group gets onto the street."

As if in response to Streight's thought, a figure appeared in the kitchen doorway.

"First two is out and away," he said loudly. A ragged cheer rose from the dancers.

"It's working!" Streight said exultantly.

A group of revelers approached Streight.

"We bin thinkin'." A short lieutenant spoke for them. "Weren't no lots drawn fer this. We all done our duty, and more, at Antietam. We reckon we're as deserving as any."

"Of course," Streight said. "And you will get your chance. We will get more men out if we send a few at a time rather than a mob that will be arrested as soon as the sun comes up."

"Or mayhap, the longer you kin keep this quiet, the better chance your friends will have goin' out this night."

"That's not the reason," Streight said indignantly.

"I ain't sayin' fer sure it is, but there's a lot o' boys here that would appreciate a chance."

"And you shall have it."

"I reckon we will," the lieutenant muttered enigmatically before leading his group back to the party.

"That is exactly why we kept this as quiet as possible for as long as possible. Everyone here is an officer, but the army has expanded so quickly many have been promoted rapidly through the ranks or got their commissions because of who they knew. They simply cannot see the benefits of long-term planning."

Walt nodded, but he did not entirely agree. Planning was all very well, but the chances of something going wrong increased dramatically as time went on. Perhaps the short lieutenant was right.

During the following half hour, men were passed through the tunnel and emerged singly and in pairs onto the Richmond streets. Walt went to the upstairs windows to watch.

The first thing he looked for was the guard. It had to be Nate. He was patrolling to Walt's left, at the end farthest from the canal, and studiously avoiding looking in that direction.

A murmur of excitement made Walt look to his right. Two figures were emerging from the building across the waste ground. With only a glance backward, they set off in deep conversation, as confidently as any legitimate citizen of the Confederate capital. The sight was thrilling.

Yet, as the two men disappeared into the night, a low groan rose from the men at the windows.

Walt noticed the short lieutenant huddled deep in conversation with a dozen or so men, making his unease with Streight's plan increase. Nevertheless, he returned to the kitchen.

There was only one batch of men left to go out, including Fleming, when a group approached Streight and Walt. The short lieutenant was in front, but there were almost thirty men with him.

"Stand aside," he said aggressively. A murmur of agreement swelled behind him.

"Wait." Streight held out his hands in a placatory gesture. "We have a plan. Everyone will get their turn in good time."

"To hell with your plan and your good time. We aim to escape this night with or without your help."

The lieutenant had raised his voice and it was beginning to draw others over to see what was going on.

Streight looked thoughtfully over the growing angry crowd. He was helpless. His only hope was to keep the situation orderly and maximize everyone's chances.

"Very well," he said, "but we must give those who have already gone the best chance."

The lieutenant looked skeptical, but he listened.

"You wait one hour before you start sending men through. No one goes in uniform. You are in charge. You send men out only two at a time. And you shut it down before sunup. Agreed?"

The lieutenant hesitated, weighing his options. Walt smiled. Putting the man in charge was a masterstroke on Streight's part. Now he was important.

"Agreed," he said eventually.

"Good. It is past nine o'clock. We have two batches still to go. You may begin at half past ten. Organize your men into pairs and make sure they have proper clothing. And the smaller the men the better. You don't want someone stuck in the tunnel."

The lieutenant hesitated for another moment, and Walt wondered if he was about to push his way through anyway, but the power of Streight's calm logic and the responsibility placed on him quieted his aggression.

"All right," he said. "Come on, you men, let's get moving here. Who has clothes that'll make 'em look like a proper southern gentleman?"

The crowd turned from mass anger to solving the individual matters of clothing and escape.

"Two batches?" Walt asked. "There is only Fleming and his companion."

Streight sighed. "That was the plan. However, I

suspect that this night will be our only chance and I plan to take it. Are you coming?"

The question took Walt by surprise — but there was no reason why not.

"Yes," he said. "I've got clothes."

"Then get them. There's not much point waiting."

Walt fled through the partyers and up the stairs to his blanket. There were still men watching the escape from the windows, but many were huddled in groups or rummaging for suitable clothes.

Walt grabbed his threadbare jacket and shoes and hurried back to the kitchen. Streight was standing by the stove talking to another officer.

"Good," he said when he saw Walt. "Captain James here has volunteered to watch over the rest, then roll back the stone in the cellar and replace the bricks in the fireplace. It won't fool any serious search, but it might give everyone a few extra hours. Come on."

In the cellar, Fleming and another man stood by the tunnel entrance. After quick handshakes with Captain James, Fleming led the way, followed immediately by his companion.

"One other thing," Streight said. "Do you know the song 'Lorena'?"

"Yes," Walt answered.

"Good. There will be a lot of escapees on the road and plenty of soldiers hunting them. It's inevitable that some groups will bump into each other. If you hear someone whistle or sing 'Lorena,' they are one of us."

Streight flashed Walt a broad smile and disappeared

into the tunnel. But Walt hesitated. He hadn't been in the tunnel since the cave-in. Now, as the black tunnel mouth loomed like a throat waiting to swallow him, he was paralyzed. If he went into that hole, the soft earth was sure to trap him. The rats would gnaw at his eyes. His breathing came in rapid gulps and a cold sweat broke out on his forehead.

"Best hurry," Captain James whispered.

Walt couldn't move.

"What's the matter? It's just a tunnel."

James grasped Walt by the shoulders and pushed him forward. Walt's body was rigid.

"Goddamn it!" James cursed. "I don't have time for this. All hell will break loose if that rabble upstairs storms the tunnel. Being shot escaping is one thing, but I don't aim to be trampled by my own comrades because I couldn't persuade a coward into the tunnel. Go or not, but get out of the way."

James turned and made his way back up the rope leading to the kitchen.

Walt took a deep breath. He wasn't a coward — or was he? He hadn't been this frightened in battle. He took one step, then another, forced his breathing to slow down. He was going to die, he was certain of that. It was a choice between a slow death by starvation and disease or a quick death in the tunnel. Walt forced the thought of rats out of his mind, but he had to think of something.

"Well, McKenzie," he said dreamily, "what do you think of all this?"

Walt ducked and entered the tunnel. "This is really quite cozy," he said. "Just like your byre."

Walt edged forward, pushing his bundle ahead of him. The floor of the tunnel had been worn smooth by the passage of so many men. Walt progressed slowly, pushing his elbows against the side walls to move forward a few inches at a time. He focused on imagining he was back on the farm, talking to McKenzie. He told her all about his adventures and the war. The more he talked, the more relaxed he became. By the time Walt felt the ground rising, he was quite calm. It was only then that he realized he had not encountered a single rat. The traffic must have scared them away.

Walt pushed his bundle out the hole and crawled after it. After the total black of the tunnel, the pale moonlight seemed bright. The shed was small, only about five feet wide and a dozen long, and was cluttered with equipment from the warehouse and offices next door. Walt could make out a chair, a desk standing on end and a pile of boxes. He could also make out a figure standing in the corner, frantically moving its hands.

"Sunday?" he whispered.

The figure nodded and stepped forward, still signing. In the poor light, Sunday's language came across as a series of barely connected words and ideas, but Walt caught most of it. "Hello, Walt. Good see again. Thought not come. Many men."

"Hello, Sunday. What are you doing in here?" Walt signed as much as he could because it was silent, but whispered the odd word he could not remember.

"I come help. Escape you."

"You're going to escape, too?"

Sunday nodded enthusiastically. "I your slave. We go north."

The idea made sense. In his panic, Walt could think only of getting through the tunnel. Being accompanied by Sunday would certainly make travel easier. Then a thought struck him. "What about Nate?"

Sunday shrugged. "He stay."

In the month Walt had lain in the prison dreaming of his journey home, he had always imagined that he would be traveling with both Sunday and Nate.

Walt slipped over to the window and peered out. Nate was patrolling slowly back and forth about five feet from the shed.

"Does he know you are here?" Walt asked.

"No. I come self."

Walt tapped lightly on the glass. Nate jumped as if he had been shot. "Nate," Walt whispered.

Nate gradually altered his route until he was beside the window. He stood with his back to the shed, surveying the open ground in front of him.

"Walt?" he whispered.

"Yes. I'm the last out of the tunnel for the time being."

"A lot came out. Where are you headed?"

Walt hesitated. He hadn't thought that far ahead and he didn't have a map. Then he remembered what the skinny officer had said.

"We'll head for the lines at Williamsburg. Across the Chickahominy at New Bridge and down the pike."

"Good. From the warehouse, follow the river to the ravine that runs northeast. That'll take you out of the city to Fair Oaks and on to New Bridge."

"Come with us."

Nate was silent.

"Sunday's coming with me."

"Sunday?"

"Yes. He was waiting in the shed for me. He wants to escape, too. If you come, we can all go north and get out of this war. They'll send me north to Canada. Sunday's an escaped slave, so they will let him come. Get rid of your uniform — we can say you're a refugee."

"I can't. It would ruin the whole thing if I left my post."

That was true enough. If Nate deserted, a hue and cry would be raised immediately, the tunnel would be discovered and the prisoners recaptured.

"You could leave tomorrow morning. Get a pass into town and follow us northeast. We won't be traveling much in daylight, so it should be easy to catch up. Whistle a tune — 'Lorena.' Do you know that one?"

"Yes."

"Then whistle it as you walk and I'll know it's you."

Nate was silent for a long time. Was this his chance? Should he go? He was about to agree when a large shadow appeared around the corner of the prison.

"You just lazing about?" Jake's voice sounded unnaturally loud after all the whispering.

Nate jerked away from the wall and stood to attention.

"All quiet," he said.

Walt shrank back from the window. Sunday grabbed his arm and signed for them to go. Walt hesitated. He hated to leave Nate, but he reluctantly followed Sunday through the door into the warehouse, brushed off as much dirt as he could, put on his jacket and shoes and prepared to go out into the street.

Signaling Sunday to stay, Walt returned to the shed window and peeked out. Nate and Jake were still deep in conversation. Nate had maneuvered so that Jake's back was to the warehouse door to the street. There was no way Nate could come now.

"Good luck, Nate," Walt whispered. Together he and Sunday slipped out the door into the night.

NATE

September 22, 1863
Libby Prison
Richmond, Virginia

Over Jake's shoulder, Nate could see two shadowy figures slip into the street and disappear. He let out an involuntary sigh of relief.

"You listenin' to me, boy?" Jake asked.

"Yes."

What his tormentor said next made his blood run cold.

"I seen your note."

"What?"

"The note that your cousin sent by the black boy near a week back. My readin' ain't that good, but it looks to me like they want you to measure some distance for them. Now, I asked myself, why would they be wantin' that? The only answer as I could find was that there's an escape in the plans."

Nate's mind was racing. Jake hadn't asked anyone to help him read the note. He'd had it for five days, yet the escape appeared to have succeeded.

"Why didn't you turn us all in?"

"That's the question, ain't it? And it belongs with a heap more questions, like why I brung your friend here and why I bin so nice to him?"

"Well?"

"The Knights of the Golden Circle."

Nate shook his head. "Who?"

"Well, it's a group thinks that this here war might not end up just the way we want. They don't want to see the noble ideals of the South die. So they're takin' *pre*cautions, as it were." Jake savored the word.

"Precautions?" Nate asked.

"Yup. *Pre*cautions. Putting something aside, as it were, so the South can rise again. Precautions against us losing the next war."

"What precautions?"

"Gold! The best precaution of all. There's stashes of coin and bullion buried all over the South and up in Canada, where no thieving Yankees can get at it. Me and Frank King was —" Something clicked in Nate's mind.

"That's why you went up to Canada. To hide gold."

"Smart boy." Jake leered, exposing stained and rotted teeth. "You didn't think we'd go all that way just fer one slave or a boy we could sell for crimp? That were a bonus. That and 'cause Frank always was one to bear a grudge. I want to help you and that young cousin of yours escape.

149

"Now, with old Frank dead at Shiloh, I'm the only one left as knows where that gold up in Canada is buried. Strikes me that travelin' with you two might be just the ticket to get me into Canada without a lot of fuss an' bother. I would surely make it worth your while."

Nate didn't believe that for a moment. Even if Jake's wild story about buried gold was true, he would never share it with Nate and Walt. But an idea was forming in Nate's mind.

"They've escaped already."

"What!" Jake raised his hand to strike Nate, but the boy held his ground and the hand dropped. "When? Who's they?"

"Walt and Sunday have gone." Nate was quite enjoying Jake's discomfort and confusion.

"Where was they goin'?"

"North."

Jake's hand raised again. "You cheeky young whelp. I ought to —"

"You ought to listen. If you want to catch them, I'll help you, but we do it my way."

Jake hesitated, torn between his natural inclination to violence and the awareness that he needed this annoying boy.

"All right," Jake said grudgingly, "but you'd best not be foolin' with me, or it'll be the worse for you."

Nate ignored the threat. "You have to find a guard to replace me. Get us some civilian clothes — in uniform they'll shoot us as deserters. And you'd better be fast. We must be out of the city well before the sun comes up."

Jake retreated toward the barracks, cursing. Nate resumed his patrol, his hands shaking with the release of tension. But he felt good. He had taken charge, stood up to Jake and begun his escape. With luck, they would overtake Walt and Sunday and make it to the Union lines and the North. Somehow, on the way, Nate would deal with Jake.

Jake returned after about fifteen minutes, carrying a pack and followed by a bleary-eyed soldier. Brusquely, he ordered the soldier to take over Nate's guard duties for the remainder of his watch. Then the odd pair marched away from the prison, skirted the neighboring warehouse and furtively doubled back to the river. In a dark alley they discarded their uniforms, and Nate, reluctantly, hid his musket — it would be impossible to carry it through the streets — but he tucked the long bayonet into his belt. Enough people carried such varied knives these days that it would not attract attention.

Their clothes were ill-fitting and mismatched. Nate had to wear his army trousers, but there were hundreds of men wandering around in all manner of rags and scraps of uniform. As they walked Richmond's late-evening streets, no one gave them a second glance.

Nate pushed the pace as hard as he could, but it was frustrating because he couldn't risk attracting attention. Even at a brisk walking pace, Jake was breathing heavily after a short distance.

Nate wanted to run because he was only sure of the first part of Walt and Sunday's route. The farther they went, the greater the chance their paths would diverge.

Nonetheless, Nate was enjoying himself. For the first time, he felt in charge of his destiny, and he liked watching Jake sweat.

By eleven, they were in the ravine, and shortly after midnight, they were struggling over the earthworks built the year before to defend Richmond against the Union attack. As there was no immediate threat, the defenses were empty, their soldiers transferred elsewhere in the beleaguered Confederacy.

Nate was beginning to fear they had missed Walt. He was moving quickly, as much to keep the laboring Jake quiet as to catch Walt. Every so often he would stop and listen, but there was nothing except the soft scurrying of small night creatures.

What would he do if they didn't catch Walt? Jake would be fairly easy to leave behind if he decided to make a break for it before daylight, but then what?

Nate whistled a few bars of "Lorena."

"Will you stop whistling that damned tune?" Jake hissed. "It's gettin' on my nerves."

Nate whistled louder. Jake took a threatening step toward him and tripped over a human skull.

WALT AND SUNDAY

September 23, 1863
Near Richmond, Virginia

Walt lay for the longest time breathing the fresh night air. He and Sunday had taken cover to watch for sentries on the defense works, but there appeared to be none. Even though the way was clear, Walt was tired, physically and emotionally. The walk through Richmond had been draining. Walt had expected every person on the street to point at him and scream "Escaped prisoner!" No one had. Except for the few who nodded politely in passing, they had all ignored him.

Once they got in the ravine, Walt's heart rate had slowed, even though he realized he was probably in greater danger. Two people skulking about in the underbrush were a lot more suspicious than a master and his slave walking along the streets, but the solitude gave him a false sense of security. He wondered what had happened to Fleming and Streight. They hadn't been far ahead, but he had no idea where they were headed. He knew some men were going to try following the river to the coast; others hoped to ride the railway out west. All Walt could do was worry about himself and Sunday — and Nate, if he decided to follow them.

Walt jumped as Sunday tapped his shoulder. "We go," he signed.

"Yes," Walt whispered back. "We'll navigate by the drinking gourd, travel at night and avoid roads and houses. Let's see if we can reach the Chickahominy River tonight."

Sunday nodded and the pair set off. Almost immediately they came to a dirt road. The moonlight was bright and the road ran straight in both directions, so Walt had little difficulty seeing that it was clear. He stepped forward, but was held back by Sunday.

"Do you see something?" he whispered.

Sunday motioned for Walt to wait. Turning around, he carefully walked backward across the road, then dropped to the ground.

Of course, Walt realized. As soon as the escape was discovered, parties would be out searching for the escapees. Footprints showing travel in the wrong direction might just put them off — if they didn't have dogs. Sunday knew all there was to know about running and hiding.

The pair traveled until about one in the morning before resting. They had crossed a couple of roads backward and waded through several streams to confuse dogs. They had just crossed a thickly tangled wood and were resting on low ground.

"Five minutes," Walt signed.

The ground was oddly irregular, as if it had been dug up recently. Here and there, white rocks gleamed palely in the moonlight. Walt reached out to the closest one. It was long, thin and cold, with a rounded end, but it didn't feel like rock. Walt tugged. With a jerk, the rock broke free of the dirt.

He was holding the end of a human thigh bone.

Walt gasped and dropped the bone — they were in the middle of a cemetery. The white rocks were human bones that had not been buried deeply enough to discourage wild animals. But Walt didn't feel scared. It was the living that frightened him, not the dead.

This must be the old battlefield of Fair Oaks, where General Silas Casey's division had been overrun by a Confederate attack. The newspapers had blamed Casey, but officers Walt had met in Libby said the disaster was because Casey had been pushed across the river without support and left to fend for himself against far superior forces. These soldiers had tried, against overwhelming odds, to stem the Confederate attack. Now they were just bones in hastily dug mass graves.

The faint sound of whistling came to Walt through the trees. Had it been "Lorena"?

"Damnation!" The curse came from Walt's right. "That's it."

Sunday touched Walt's arm and indicated that they

should crawl away to their left. Walt shook his head. The voice sounded vaguely familiar, but it was hoarse and breathy, as if its owner had been running.

"You don't know where we're goin', and I've had enough."

Walt and Sunday recognized Jake Stone's voice just as they heard Nate say, "They came this way. They can't be far ahead of us."

"I don't believe you no more, boy. You tell me the truth or, so help me, I'll blow yer brains out alongside these poor bones."

Walt heard the unmistakable sound of a hammer being cocked. Instinctively, he yelled, "Nate! Over here."

The noise of a brief scuffle was followed by a large figure looming out of the shadows. Walt got to his feet as Jake lumbered toward him, a Colt revolver in his right hand.

"So, we've found you. You're my ticket, boy. I'll make you rich fer it."

"Don't believe him!" Nate shouted from behind Jake. "He has some cock-and-bull story about buried gold, but even if it exists, he doesn't plan to share it."

"I don't need you no more," Jake said, turning and leveling the revolver in Nate's direction. "I thank you fer leading me here, but yer just useless baggage now."

Nate dived to his right and hurled something long and silver at Jake. Jake's Colt crashed and Nate screamed. His body spun awkwardly and landed heavily.

Time slowed for Walt. He saw Nate fall and he saw the bayonet spiral through the air, knock the revolver from Jake's hand and embed itself in the ground.

Rolling forward, Walt grabbed the handle of the bayonet and pulled it free. Holding it in two hands, he rose to his feet, stabbing up toward Jake's ample belly.

Jake was quick for a big man. He made a grab for Walt and clamped his strong hands painfully over Walt's wrists, holding the bayonet away from his body.

The two men stood facing each other, the butt of the bayonet digging painfully into Walt's stomach and the point wavering an inch or two from Jake. Walt's arms were paralyzed.

Jake leered down at him. "Aimin' to be brave, are you, boy? Think a pip-squeak like you can gut old Jake?"

Walt resisted the hands twisting his wrists, but very slowly, the bayonet point was being forced away from its target.

"You just let go o' this bayonet, then you 'n me can head off to your home and dig up the gold that's buried 'neath the old burned cowshed. There's enough there fer all of us, so I'll just take my share and skedaddle. What do you say to that, boy? You want to be rich?"

Walt was amazed that Stone thought some gold could outweigh the past. Angrily, he pushed on the bayonet. It was no good.

"You best stay, boy, if'n you know what's good fer you. I reckon old Frank gave you a cut or two. If you don't want me to add to them, you'd best step back."

Walt looked up at Stone, who was looking angrily over his shoulder. Sunday must be behind him, but what was he doing?

Jake's expression turned from anger to puzzlement. "Keep back, boy."

Walt saw Sunday's arms reach around him and grab Jake's jacket and felt Sunday's breath on his neck.

There was a look of fear in Jake's eyes now.

"Git back now, boy."

Gradually, Walt felt Sunday apply pressure to his back by pulling on Jake's clothing. The bayonet edged forward. Walt pushed with all his might, and the point slowly disappeared through Jake's shirt. The big man gasped and clenched his hands tighter. The veins in his forehead stood out like ropes and his eyes were wild.

"We can share the gold," he said through shallow breathing. "There's plenty fer everyone."

Another inch of the bayonet entered his stomach.

Jake's breathing was coming in short, hoarse gulps. A gurgling sound came from somewhere deep within him.

Then, all of a sudden, the hands relaxed. The bayonet drove hard up beneath his rib cage.

A surprised look replaced the terror on Jake's face. A terrible wet bubbling sound came from him and a red froth spilled over his lips and covered his chin.

Walt screamed and pushed backward. Sunday's grip broke. The three bodies tumbled to the ground. Walt lay shivering as waves of nausea swept over him. He turned, only to find himself looking into Jake Stone's dead, staring eyes.

Walt pushed himself to his feet. Sunday was already standing, looking over at Nate, his brow furrowed in concentration as he struggled to decide what to do next. Walt rushed over to his cousin and knelt by him.

Nate lay, groaning and clutching his bloodstained thigh. Walt tried to rip the heavy trouser material to see what damage Jake's bullet had done.

"I need a knife!" he yelled, turning to Sunday.

Sunday placed a foot on Jake's chest and pulled the bayonet free. After rapidly wiping the worst of the gore on Jake's jacket, he handed the blade to Walt, who sliced open Nate's trouser leg.

The bullet had cut a deep gouge on the outside of Nate's right thigh but had missed the bone. It was bleeding freely, but there was no sign of the pumping that would have indicated a severed artery.

Walt cleaned pieces of material out of the wound as best he could and bound it tightly with the severed trouser leg. By the time he had finished, Nate had stopped groaning and was trying to sit up. He looked pale but was taking an interest in Walt's work.

"How bad is it?"

"The bone's okay and the bleeding has almost stopped. How do you feel?"

"Weak, but the pain's less now. What happened to Jake?"

"He's dead."

Nate nodded silently. He looked from Walt to Sunday.

"We're back together again," he said flatly.

"Yes," Walt replied. But none of them was the same person they had been a year and a half ago at Shiloh.

WALT, SUNDAY

AND NATE

September 27, 1863
Williamsburg Pike, Virginia

Walt didn't care what happened to him. He was filthy, hungry and exhausted, and he just wanted to rest. Five days and nights of walking, hiding and being terrified had drained him. There had been close calls — when they had lain in a thicket scared to breathe as Confederate cavalry scoured the woods around them — and unexpected kindnesses. The widow of a soldier killed at Shiloh had taken them in, tended to Nate's wound and given them all a hot meal.

Nate had used his southern accent to talk them onto a ferry over the Chickahominy River, Sunday had found them a slave to lead them back onto the right road after they'd become hopelessly lost, and Walt's knowledge of the woods had kept them out of the way of search parties.

The traveling had been slow because of Nate's leg, but he had borne up well and the wound showed no signs of infection. But now they had reached the end. It was dusk and they lay on the embankment by the Williamsburg Pike.

"It can't be far now."

"To where, Walt?" Nate asked tiredly.

"To the Union lines."

"And then where?"

It was a question Walt had been thinking about. He was going home, that was certain. If any doubts had remained after the lynching in New York, they had disappeared at the sight of Jake's face. It was one thing to see men killed in battle or even see them murdered at a distance. It was quite another to feel a man's last breath on your face — even a man as twisted as Jake Stone. Walt doubted he would ever be able to kill anything again, man or beast. He thought back to an old story his father had told him about a dying American soldier in the War of 1812. The experience had scarred his father and turned him against war forever. Now Walt understood.

But what about the others?

"Home," Walt said.

"You have a home."

"So do you. If you want it."

Sunday signed at some length.

"What'd he say?" Nate asked.

"He said that he's going to the farm. All he wants is to work Touss's old place in peace. Come with us. The Confederacy's finished. It might take another year, or even two, but it's just senseless killing from now on."

"It's all senseless killing," Nate said bleakly.

"Then come to the farm."

"I don't know."

Sunday pointed to the three of them, picked up the sturdy forked stick Nate used as a crutch and scratched in the dirt. The word "family" appeared in rough letters.

Walt burst out laughing. "You're hopeless, Sunday. Family has an 'i' in it."

Nate caught the infection of the laugh and joined in. Once he started, he couldn't stop. He threw an arm around Walt, as much to stop himself from falling over as in companionship. The pair laughed like idiots until tears were streaming down their cheeks. Sunday watched, a broad smile on his face.

"We'll all buy shovels," Nate said between gasps for breath, "and dig up Jake Stone's gold."

"We'll dig up the whole county." Their laughter became almost hysterical.

Again Sunday scratched in the dirt — "cowshed."

"What's that?" Nate asked when he had calmed down.

"Of course!" Walt yelled. "I'd forgotten. Stone mentioned the burned cowshed in the fight. If there really is gold, that's where it is."

"Then let's go and get it."

Walt and Nate were making so much noise they didn't hear the cavalry patrol until it was almost upon them. The clanking of horses' bits, frighteningly close, finally silenced them. The three lay in the darkness, barely daring to breathe.

"Who are you?" a disembodied voice asked.

"Three travelers," Walt said as noncommittally as possible.

"Step forward and be identified."

Walt and the others rose unsteadily and shambled toward shadowy figures on horseback, Nate leaning heavily on Sunday. The cavalry fanned out and surrounded them. Walt's heart sank. It was so unfair.

One of the soldiers began to sing. He had a rough voice, but it was oddly suited to the mournful refrain.

"The years creep slowly by, Lorena
The snow is on the grass again
The sun's low down the sky, Lorena
The frost gleams where the flowers have been."

"You're Union!" Walt exclaimed.

"Indeed we are," a familiar voice said. "And, I suppose, you will try to tell me that you are in fact Lieutenant Andrew Davis and not Walter McGregor, a foreign national?"

"Captain Fleming! What are you doing here?"

"Streight and I arrived two days back and have been bringing in escapees. I see you have brought Sunday, but who is the other?"

"My cousin, Nate McGregor. He is wounded in the leg."

"Then we'd best see to him."

Walt watched things happen as if through a veil. He was safe. He was going home. Someone else could make decisions from now on. Thoughts of the farm and a simple life flooded his mind and he had to fight back tears. The first thing he would do when he got back to Cornwall, he promised himself, was tell his father he had been right about a peaceful life in a quiet backwater.

Nate's leg throbbed and his emotions were all confused. He didn't feel the joy that was obviously washing over his cousin. He was safe and, with luck, could look forward to a new life in Canada — but it wouldn't be easy settling on the farm. It would be a very different life. The world Nate had grown up in was gone, destroyed by secession and war. It would be better to begin a new life in a new place, rather than in the ruins of the Confederacy. At least he had a family now to help him.

Sunday released Nate to the care of a couple of soldiers and flexed his stiff muscles. He, too, was heading home. From being a runaway slave with a price on his head, he had become a free soldier and a free man. The Emancipation Proclamation and the Battle at Fort Wagner had forever changed the way he would be looked upon, but the struggle was far from over. Sunday would help in that struggle, but quietly and peacefully.

The broad historical events of the story — Gettysburg, Fort Wagner, the New York Draft Riots — are accurately portrayed; however, some details have been altered to fit. For instance, Libby Prison was a real place. Its layout is based on maps, photos and descriptions by prisoners. The most famous escape in the Civil War did happen there, but I have moved it to September 1863 from February 9, 1864. One hundred and nine prisoners escaped that night through a tunnel. Fifty-seven made it safely to the Union lines. The rest were recaptured, although the bodies of two were found floating in the James River.

After the war, Libby returned to being a warehouse, until, in 1889, it was dismantled and rebuilt in Chicago as a tourist attraction. Unfortunately, the hole in the wall touted as the famous tunnel entrance was put in the wrong place. A few bricks and a door in a museum are all that remain of Libby Prison today.

Some characters are fictional composites of real people. Most notably, the exploits of Nathan Hanson Woods are based on those of two Confederate raiders, Nathan Bedford Forrest, who survived the war to found the Ku Klux Klan, and John Hanson McNeill, who raided in northwest Virginia. Colonel Abel Streight and the Lightning Mule Brigade did exist, and Streight was one of those who successfully escaped from Libby.

Even today, there are stories of buried Confederate gold in Canada.

ACKNOWLEDGMENTS

As with *The Flags of War*, which describes the earlier adventures of Nate, Walt and Sunday, Bruce Catton's trilogy, *The Centennial History of the Civil War*, and Ken Burns's television documentary and book, *The Civil War*, provided much background. The story of Libby Prison is told in Diane Swanson's *Tunnels*. "Civil War Richmond," an online research project, has a remarkable collection of primary documents, photographs and maps pertaining to Richmond, Virginia, during the Civil War. Again, Charis Wahl has smoothed the wrinkles, excised my sloppiness and encouraged me to make the story all it could be.